THE VICIOUS SWANS

And Other Tall Tales

SCOTT TILLEY

The Vicious Swans
And Other Tall Tales

Copyright © 2017 Scott Tilley

Cover design © Scott Tilley

Cover photograph © Vaclav Volrab/Shutterstock

Published by the Anthology Alliance

**Anthology
Alliance**

An imprint of Precious Publishing, LLC

Precious Publishing
www.PreciousPublishing.biz

ISBN-13: 978-0-9979456-8-3

ISBN-13: 978-0-9979456-9-0 (ebook)

TABLE OF CONTENTS

DEDICATION

To scribblers everywhere.

PREFACE

I've been writing for as long as I can remember. My first efforts were summaries of "Star Trek" books I was reading while at the beach. I was probably ten years old or so. Ironically, last year I revisited the "Star Trek" world in a series of public lectures to celebrate the 50th anniversary of the fantastic franchise.

This book contains a collection of short stories I wrote between 2004 and 2014. Some of the stories have a serious theme, such as living well with diabetes, but most of them are meant to be more lighthearted. What do you do upon finding a huge spider in the bathroom just inches from your face when you are sitting down to business? What's it like to struggle with unfamiliar technology (such as a malfunctioning electronic fob to start a car) while freezing in the depths of winter? How would you react when attacked by rampaging swans? They may look cute, but they're vicious beasts. Don't let anyone tell you otherwise!

I hope you enjoy this collection. More information about my other books and writing activities is available online at www.amazon.com/author/stilley.

Scott Tilley
Melbourne, FL
July 31, 2017

ACKNOWLEDGMENTS

I've used some of these stories as part of my attempts at stand-up comedy. Thanks to everyone who's had to suffer through some rough deliveries. Making people laugh is a lot harder than it looks.

Thanks to members of the Brevard Scribblers for providing constructive feedback on early drafts of these stories. Some of them were only in bullet format when I first read them aloud. I've learned that hearing your words spoken is a great way of improving the written word.

I joined the Scribblers when I first moved to Florida in 2003 and I've been a member ever since. I would encourage all aspiring writers to join a local support group. Feedback from fellow authors (however difficult to accept) and their camaraderie (always easy to accept) makes the solitary task of writing much more enjoyable.

Lastly, I'm grateful that we live in a world full of colorful people. Many of these stories are based on experiences I've had while traveling the globe. Some of these experiences were not much fun at the time, but writing about them sure was.

LIFELONG COMPANION

April 2004

"34.4."

Silence.

"Are you sure?"

"There's no mistake. Your readings are more than 500 percent above normal."

"What would you say if I told you I lied about my symptoms? That I didn't really have any of them?"

"I'd say the same thing: you have diabetes."

* * *

In early October 1993 I had been in Montréal for a conference. All that week I had been thirsty. When the conference was over I spent the weekend visiting with my parents. Since they live in Montréal and I lived in Victoria, I didn't get to see them very often. I remember getting up every night to get several glasses of water and being very tired all the time. I could barely keep my eyes open in the afternoons. However, I put it down to travel, hard work, and lack of sleep.

I went to Waterloo for another conference the following week, hoping things would improve. They got worse. I was drinking all the time. In the evening, after the conference sessions had finished, I would go out and purchase four or five bottles of water, pop, anything to slake my thirst. And I was still feeling wiped out.

I returned to Victoria on a Friday night. My wife met me at the airport. I jokingly told her "I think I have diabetes." Of course, I was not serious. There was no way I had just 'come down' with diabetes like it was some kind of head cold or something. Only older overweight people get it. Right?

On Sunday afternoon I played soccer as usual. Well, I tried to play as usual. Actually, I could barely lift my feet and put one step in front of another; running around a soccer field for two hours was impossible. I spent most of the match sitting on the sidelines, half in a stupor, wondering what was wrong with me. Did I really have diabetes?

Early next week I had to visit my doctor to get a prescription refill for my arthritis medication. Almost as an afterthought, I told him my experiences and symptoms of the past two weeks. I had also lost over 12 pounds from going to the toilet all the time. "Probably just a bug," he said. "But we'll do a blood test, just in case." This was at 11:00 am. He phoned me at 5:00 pm with the news: my blood glucose readings were 34.4; the normal range is 4 to 6. I had it all right.

I hung up the phone and sat on the couch, staring into space. Diabetes? Me? What did I know about diabetes? Blindness, kidney disease, and strokes: all these terrible complications flashed through my mind. I remember thinking at the time what a weird coincidence it was that my father suffers from rheumatoid arthritis, and my grandfather was diabetic—yet I'm adopted. What are the chances of that happening I wondered?

Then it started to hit me what a change being a diabetic would make in my life. "Let's start right away," my doctor had said. "Come in tomorrow morning, and I'll explain what diabetes mellitus is all about. We'll discuss blood sugars and I'll teach you how to measure them. Next week we'll start with the insulin injections." I spent that evening sitting at home, nervous and worried. What was in store for me?

* * *

My doctor is a no-nonsense kind of guy. When I walked into his office the next day, without any preamble, he explained that there are two types of diabetes: Type I (which used to be called juvenile diabetes), and Type II (which used to be called adult-onset diabetes). By far the most common is Type II, which afflicts about 95% of diabetics. They can usually control their blood sugars by losing weight, altering their diet to eat healthier foods with less refined sugar, and taking special pills that help their body process insulin more effectively.

Type I diabetics are much less common (about 5%), and they have a more difficult time. In a Type I diabetic, the body's immune system destroys the islets in the pancreas that make insulin; there is no insulin produced at all. Without insulin, your body can't metabolize glucose (the source of energy for your cells), and eventually, you die. When my doctor told me this, I knew what was coming next: he told me I was a Type I (insulin dependent) diabetic. I would need to learn how to give myself a needle several times a day for the rest of my life. Wonderful.

But first I would need to learn how to use the glucose monitor to test my blood sugars (which I need to do four times a day). This involves pricking your finger with a spring-loaded lancet to draw a sample of blood, which is then placed onto a small stick and inserted into a machine about the size of a pager. In twenty seconds or so your blood glucose reading is shown on the tiny display. The first time I did it, it hurt like hell. I had set the spring too tight, causing the lancet to pierce the tender flesh on the tip of my ring finger too deeply. The glucose reading wasn't very encouraging either: 28.8.

The next visit to the doctor was the biggie: needles. I had been told that in the past people learned how to inject themselves by first practicing on an orange. It wasn't that way for me. After explaining the injection sites to me (arms, thighs, stomach, and buttocks), my doctor dropped his pants and sat down. I looked at him in surprise, slightly amused, wondering what he was going to do. This was the first time I've ever been in a doctor's office where the patient was dressed and the doctor was disrobed.

He took a syringe and vial from a drawer, drew a few units of clear liquid from the vial into the needle, and proceeded to plunge it into his thigh. He pushed down on the plunger until the liquid disappeared from the needle into his leg. "That's all there is to it," he said. Whereupon he stood up, pulled up his pants, and promptly stumbled to his desk. "That was a topical analgesic, not real insulin; it put my leg to sleep," he smirked. "When you use insulin yourself later today, this won't happen." Well, that's good to know I thought, wondering if the needle hurt much. (It did. And it still does. Every time.)

* * *

Within one week I found myself turned into a human pin-cushion: taking small blood samples four times a day to test the glucose levels, and injecting insulin twice a day. Add this to the twice-a-day pill popping for my arthritis and I was feeling more than a little bit sorry for myself. Here I was, not even thirty yet, and a walking drugstore.

The diabetic diet is one that is low in sugar, salt, and fats, and high in fiber. In other words, it's a diet that everyone should follow—and that almost no one does. It's not like you can choose a diet to lose weight and follow it for three months; this is a diet for life. I now think of meals mainly in terms of carbohydrate exchanges, all in the attempt to maintain a constant glucose level and let my synthetic insulin do its work.

But sometimes it does its work too well. The result is hypoglycemia: sweats, shakes, dizziness, and the genuine need to gulp down some sugar fast. Too much insulin causes your body to burn its sugar stores faster than it should, dropping the glucose level. Your body recognizes this as a serious condition and releases adrenaline in an attempt to shore up its energy. It takes at least fifteen minutes for these reactions to subside.

The opposite end of the spectrum is hyperglycemia: high blood sugar. With Type I diabetics, there is no natural insulin in the body, so glucose cannot penetrate cells to be used as energy. The body needs energy from somewhere, so it burns fat instead. But the fat is only partially burned, leaving ketones in the blood. The result is diabetic ketoacidosis. If left untreated, the situation rapidly deteriorates and can lead to coma. So I guess giving myself daily insulin injections is not that bad after all.

* * *

It's now over 11 years since I was first diagnosed as diabetic. My blood sugars are close to normal most of the time. I'm on a strict regime to maintain these levels, but things could be worse. I suppose I should feel relieved that I don't have inoperable brain cancer or AIDS or something even more horrible.

Diabetes is a chronic disease that as yet has no cure. It's my

lifelong companion. But as with all long-term companions, you grow
accustomed to them.

# # #

BLENDING THE BEST OF POINDEXTER AND GEKKO

July 2008

In late May I attended the "Google I/O" conference in San Francisco (http://code.google.com/events/io/). I was there to learn more about the Google platform for Web application development. In particular, I was interested in seeing how we could leverage open technologies and new capabilities provided by companies like Google in our core programming and software engineering courses at Florida Tech.

With nearly 3,000 people milling around, many booths crowded with people watching demonstrations, and attendees reading their email while lounging on bean bag chairs scattered all over the floor, Moscone Center was a bustling place. Between sessions, I wandered over to the Information kiosk and asked a lovely lady who worked for Google how I could get copies of the presentations. She looked at me, smiled, and then read a hand-written note that told me the presentations would be available next week as Google Docs on the conference Web site and as videos on YouTube. Then she said, "I hope you understand what that means. I don't. I guess you can tell that I'm from another generation." I thought about her comment for a moment, smiled back, and replied, "I think I am too."

Now don't get me wrong – I'm not that long in the tooth. But the reality is that technology is changing so fast that it's incredibly difficult for the average person to keep up. Blogs. Podcasts. Facebook. AJAX. Android. Flex. Ruby on Rails. Google Gears. Cloud Computing. IPTV. Digg. Tumblr. Twitter. These aren't just acronyms or catch phrases: they are examples of recent innovations that are having a significant impact on our society. And to be successful today, you need to understand them from both technical and business perspectives.

In many ways, it's easier to understand these new developments from a technical point of view. The trick is being able to separate the hype from the reality. Some of these are truly revolutionary; others are just new names for old ideas. This is where the value of a solid education becomes apparent. Learning critical thinking skills to perform analytical analysis is one of the most important things I try to instill in our students. While at the Google I/O conference I could see that many of the young developers in the audience were incredibly impressed by some of the things they were hearing, while I was sitting there thinking that I've listened to a lot of this before. Several times in fact. But it's only through experience that one can place innovative ideas in historical context. Learning how to program in Java or C# might be important today, but knowing how to learn new programming languages very rapidly is more important for tomorrow.

From a business point of view, some of these new developments will facilitate new business models. For example, we may be at a tipping point when it comes to Web-based applications, and if so, this would have profound implications for companies that make most of their revenue from PC-based applications (e.g., Microsoft). Companies like Google are shaking the very foundations of established industries through their advertising-driven business model. Most, if not all, of the software discussed at the Google I/O conference is pretty good (and getting better all the time), it's open source, and it's free; how can an older company compete with that?

To thrive as a young professional in today's global marketplace, particularly in a high-tech area like Brevard County and the Space Coast, you need to have the inquisitive scientific mind of Poindexter and the unrelenting competitive drive of Gordon Gekko. You must have the business acumen to know how to translate technical advances into commercial success. It's certainly not easy to be adept in either field; having a good mix of the two is even more challenging. Perhaps instead of the negative stereotypes of Poindexter and Gekko, a better model for success would be the inspirational giants of the Renaissance, such as Leonardo da Vinci and Michelangelo, but upgraded to Version 2.

# # #

Committee Time

August 2008

Time to Serve

There comes a time in everyone's life when the call comes to serve on a committee. Or a few committees; it seems the word spreads very quickly that you're "available."

If this is your first time, your reaction might well be one of pride. In some ways, being asked to serve on a committee is an acknowledgment by your peers that your opinion is valued and your judgment is sound. As an optimist, you would view being asked to serve on a committee as an honor and a privilege. Of course you can make the time to serve – glad to do it!

On the other hand, if you've served on several committees in the past, your reaction might be quite different. Over time your outlook may change from optimistic to pessimistic. What was once an honor and a privilege has now become a chore and a bother. And who has the time?

Do You Have the Time?

The irony is that the people most capable of serving on committees effectively are those with the least amount of time available to do so. It seems new tasks are added to the list all the time, but very few are ever taken off. At some point, even the most organized person reaches their limit and spends more time churning than doing.

Time is the most valuable commodity we have, so giving it to someone else is a precious gift. This is especially so in today's 24/7 world, where everyone seems rushed all the time. If you say "yes" to serving on a committee, then you are implicitly saying "no" to something else. Only you know which activity is more important.

When you are young and time seems endless, serving on a committee can be seen as a good use of your time. As you get a little older, your priorities change. You eventually realize that learning to say "no" is a very valuable skill.

Serving Time

The more people involved in the decision-making process, the longer it takes. Things become even more complicated when the committee members are scattered across different time zones, living on different continents, and with different work ethics. In such situations, many committee meetings are virtual: email, instant messages, and telephone calls replace face-to-face interactions. The asynchronous nature of these meetings often means that reaching consensus on anything begins to seem impossible.

I've spent a good part of the last two years leading a large committee of over 100 people from all over the world. I find myself awake nearly every night at 4:00 am, sending email to China to make sure they get the messages before their business day ends, sending email to Italy to make sure they get the messages before their business day begins, and chatting with friends in Canada who are working all night every night no matter what.

Some committee members follow "German time," which means things are done strictly on schedule. Other people follow "Greek time" (or "Jamaican time"), which has a much more relaxed attitude towards deadlines. I follow my own time, which I adjust as needed.

Over the last 20 years, I've served on dozens of committees. I've enjoyed the experience of serving on this one too, but I think once is enough. Everyone should serve their time, but eventually, you should get paroled.

# # #

THE NATURAL

September 2008

Immigrant

The immigration facility in the Port Angeles, WA airport is tiny. Just one officer was staffing the desk, which meant the line was quite long. I'd gone through Customs & Immigration many times in the past when I crossed the border, but this time it was different. When I was asked, "What is the purpose of your visit?" I didn't answer with the usual reply of "I'm going to a conference." This time, I said, "I'm moving to the U.S." That simple statement certainly got the officer's attention. And it marked the formal start of my journey to citizenship.

I was entering the country on a J-1 ("Visiting Scholar") visa. Before I contemplated moving to the U.S. I knew very little about the immigration process. Now I know quite a lot. In fact, I know more about the U.S. system than I do the Canadian system since I've been forced to deal with more of the issues here. About the only thing I knew about the J-1 visa is that it is a "quality" visa, which meant I had no trouble at the border. I was in. But I was now an "immigrant," a term that usually brings images of the Statue of Liberty or dusty desert border towns; my image was a rainy little office in the Pacific Northwest.

Interestingly, my immigration experience is far more common than you think. It's true that the illegal type makes the news more often. But legal immigration is still the preferred route for most people, and since immigrants founded this country, I have a lot of good historical company. So maybe being called an "immigrant" (for a while at least) is not so bad.

Alien

After you spend some time here, the next step was to apply for a "green card," which is more properly called a "resident alien" card. I never liked the connotations of the word "immigrant" very much; I liked the word "alien" even less.

It's a strange name, "alien." It doesn't exactly make you feel welcome. Other countries call you a "landed immigrant" or something similar. Here, I was an alien, an outsider, literally someone from another place, who currently resided in the country.

The American Heritage Dictionary defines the word "alien" as follows:

American Heritage Dictionary - _Cite This Source_ - _Share This_
a·li·en ◀)) (ā'lē-ən, āl'yən) Pronunciation Key
adj.
1. Owing political allegiance to another country or government; foreign: _alien residents_.
2. Belonging to, characteristic of, or constituting another and very different place, society, or person; strange. See Synonyms at foreign.
3. Dissimilar, inconsistent, or opposed, as in nature: _emotions alien to her temperament_.

n.
1. An unnaturalized foreign resident of a country. Also called _noncitizen_.
2. A person from another and very different family, people, or place.
3. A person who is not included in a group; an outsider.
4. A creature from outer space: _a story about an invasion of aliens_.
5. _Ecology_ An organism, especially a plant or animal, that occurs in or is naturalized in a region to which it is not native.

Yuck. Who wants to be characterized in that way? I didn't. But it's the next step in the process. So I applied for my green card, which was a very laborious task. It took a mountain of paperwork and nearly two years to complete – and even then I was on the accelerated program: "in the national interest."

When my green card (which is actually pink) arrived, I was

thrilled. I was now an official "resident," which I prefer to "alien." But I wanted more: I wanted to be a citizen.

Citizen

You must be a resident alien for at least five years before you can apply for U.S. citizenship. I waited for nearly ten. I even had to renew my green card during this time. (Green cards used to be good for life; now they are only good for ten years.) But in July 2007 I finally got all of my paperwork together and submitted my application for citizenship. The most time-consuming portion of the application process was accounting for every one of my trips abroad since I became a resident alien. Given all the traveling I do, the trip list went on for quite a few pages.

In late Spring of 2008 I received a formal notice from the INS to appear for fingerprinting. A few months later another notice arrived, telling me to appear for an interview and a civics exam. I studied all of the material; I knew the answers to all 96 questions in the study guide.

Question 15: Who elects the President of the United States?

Answer 15: The Electoral College

Question 20: What are the three branches of our government?

Answer 20: Executive, Judicial, and Legislative

Question 24: Who elects Congress?

Answer 24: The citizens of the United States

I was asked ten questions during the hour-long interview. I only stumbled on the last one: I said "the people of the U.S." I should have been more explicit: "the **citizens** of the U.S." But no matter, I passed. I was now a citizen too!

I attended the naturalization ceremony in July of this year. I was given a small flag, a letter from the President, and a certificate with my photo on it. There were about 195 people in the ceremony from 53 different countries, from literally all over the world, A-Z.

My long journey had started with a stamp in my old passport, marking me as an "immigrant." In the middle of the process I was an "alien." It finally ended a few weeks after the ceremony with a brand new passport. I was now a "natural."

* * *

PS: My first election is coming up. Who can convince me not to cancel their vote? ☺

# # #

THE BEECHES OF BEIJING

October 2008

Beijing

Beijing is the capital of the People's Republic of China. It is a huge city of 17 million people. The size of Beijing dwarfs even the largest US cities most of us are familiar with, such as New York and Los Angeles. The scale of this modern metropolis is like nothing else I've ever seen or experienced. It truly is a vision of the future.

When you drive down one of Beijing's many crowded highways, it sometimes seems like all 1.3 billion Chinese people are on the road with you. The lanes are clogged with cars, trucks, buses, bicycles, and even the occasional donkey cart. But there is almost never a traffic accident. It's amazing to see how the drivers control their vehicles with surgical precision, weaving in and out, coming within a hair's width of others but never quite touching. Driving there is not for the faint of heart. I use cabs.

If you've ever lived in a large city, you know that the hustle and bustle of daily life can eventually become tiring. Dealing with the crowds, the noise, and the chaos – it all starts to become bothersome. Even short trips to the store require a lot of energy. One longs for a respite from it all, a quiet place to go, a little hideaway to be alone for a while. I found such a place: the beaches of Beijing.

Beaches

Most people don't associate Beijing with beaches. But they are there. Hidden away in different parts of the city are parks, and inside the parks are the beaches. They are an unexpected oasis that instills a feeling of peacefulness and tranquility.

During a recent trip to China, I was staying at the Beijing

Friendship Hotel. It's located inside the third ring of the city (there are five rings in Beijing) and is the largest garden hotel in Asia. The complex is so large that there are over 20 restaurants just within the hotel grounds.

As I stood on the balcony of my room, I was looking at one of the beeches. It stood in stark contrast to the skyscrapers that surround the hotel. As the wind blew in from the Gobi desert, the beeches' leaves made a soothing fluttering sound. Magpies hopped from branch to branch, and from tree to tree. Somehow the bedlam from the city outside faded away, replaced by the calming beeches of Beijing.

* * *

I'm not sure they are actually beech trees. But somehow, other tree names, such as Poplar or Spruce, don't lend themselves well to this story.

#

SNOW REMOVAL

April 2009

When I Was Young

When I was growing up in Montréal, I spent a good part of my time in the winter outdoors, playing ice hockey, skiing, and shoveling snow. The first two activities were fun; the last one definitely was not. There were a few people in the neighborhood that had snow blowers, but they weren't as common as they are today. Mostly it was the young boys like me who performed snow removal.

I never liked doing it. Our driveway was long, and the house is on a corner – which means extra snow gets dumped there from the plow as it goes by after a snowstorm (the plow shows no mercy). It often took over two hours to shovel the whole driveway, the path, the back door, and the steps. And even in the deep cold (-30F and windy), it was sweaty work.

But snow removal was also an opportunity to earn some extra money. After finishing my driveway, I would often head out to the neighbors and ask if I could shovel their driveway for $5. Sometimes I would share the task with my friend, which made the work go faster.

Today

I no longer live in the cold weather, and snow removal is usually a distant memory. However, this year I've had to travel back up to the Great White North twice during the wintertime. These two visits made the snow removal problem very personal again. And it illustrated how times have changed.

My parents are now too old to shovel the driveway by themselves (although they often forced to do a little themselves – otherwise they are locked in their house). So they rely on outside services. What's amazing is how many different services are now needed to replace one little boy.

When there is just a lite dusting of snow, a broom is usually enough to sweep the path. My folks can still do this themselves (although the ice makes it slippery work). But since snow seems to be falling almost every day, even this relatively simple clearing becomes wearisome by April.

When there is more snow on the ground, and more falling all the time, the broom is not enough. My parents have a yearly contract for a tractor to take care of the driveway. But this usually means checking the front window every hour, waiting for the tractor to arrive. It only takes two minutes for the tractor to move the snow and large bounders from the driveway to the lawn (leaving another problem for Spring when the snow starts to melt). The snow banks are piled over 7' high, making backing out of the driveway very exciting. But the tractor doesn't do the stairs, the path, or the back door and patio. So another service is needed.

My parents have another contract with a young university student who works "old school": he uses a shovel to clear the stairs, the path, and the back door and patio. He also uses a scoop to remove the snow from the top of the carport (it has a soft roof and would cave in if the snow was not clear off of it – which has happened in the past). But like the tractor, the student works on his own schedule. This means my parents are often stuck in the house, waiting for the snow to be cleared before they can get out. Many times the snow is so deep that they can't even walk to the road, never mind get the car out of the driveway.

In the Future

What can be done to make the situation better in the future? Besides moving to Florida, I mean. Services of any kind are getting harder to come by; not too many students are willing to work for a few bucks (and it's $25 now, not the $5 I used to get for the whole driveway).

Some people have installed heaters in the concrete of their driveway. This does help keep the surface clear, but when the snow really falls, it's not a good solution. In 2008 there were nine major snowstorms that dumped over 350cm (138" or 11.5') on the city. That's a lot of shoveling.

I did a fair amount of shoveling myself during my visits this year. But that's not a viable solution either since I'm not there very often. And I still don't like it…

A friend once told me: "Don't go north of Titusville in the wintertime." Good advice.

# # #

THE BUICK IN THE BATHROOM

April 2009

Wakey Wakey!

I had just returned from yet another road trip. After unpacking and cleaning up I went to bed, tired from the plane ride and the long day in the nation's capital. Sometime around 3:00 am I got up to go to the toilet. It was then that I met the Buick in the bathroom. (Apologies to Woody Allen in "Annie Hall.")

Somewhat groggy, I was standing "at the ready." I reached out with my left had to switch on the light and stopped just short of the switch. There was a large brown … something … stuck to the wall, just below the empty towel rack.

As often happens in unexpected or emergency situations, I stood there, dumbfounded, unable to move. One hand was tightening around my equipment; the other was outstretched and frozen. After a few moments, I woke up. Fully. Then I quietly crept out of the bathroom, wondering what to do next.

Photo ID

What I did was take a picture. Maybe I needed proof that what I was looking at was real. It was. Very real. It was a giant spider approximately the size of a Buick – with legs nearly as long as my outstretched hand (see photo below). I'm no entomologist, but I can scientifically describe this spider as nasty.

(Later on, I looked online to determine the type of spider that was threatening me. It was a Brown Recluse, which is venomous. Its bite can cause necrosis in the flesh, leaving a deep gash. I have since dropped off the corpse to the biology department at the university for confirmation.)

Some people don't like snakes. I'm a little squeamish about spiders. As a boy I used to collect Daddy Long Legs in jars – maybe they were getting back at me.

I crept back out of the bathroom and wondered what to do. I decided that the photo was enough to immortalize the Buick – it could now "go away." And I'd help it out.

The Chase

The problem was that the Buick was too big to squish. So I rushed downstairs and grabbed a can of roach spray, hoping that it was also lethal to sedan-sized arachnids. Then I stepped back into the spider's lair.

The first blast from the can caused the spider to leap from one wall to another, landing just above the toilet. I swear I could hear the spider's leg "thump" as it hit the wall and scuttled down towards the floor. This caused me to jump out of the bathroom, since I had belated remembered that my feet were still bare (and I felt my equipment might pose too tempting a target for the spider's next leap). All I could think of was the face hugger scenes from the movie "Alien."

After I got dressed, I moved back into the bathroom, can at the ready. I let loose with several blasts, chasing the spider across the walls, around the floor, and into the tub. Eventually, the Buick ran out of gas and it stalled near my foot. The spider's heart might have stopped, but mine was pounding enough for the both of us.

Traumatized

Everyone has heard stories about snakes in toilet bowls. I know someone who encountered one personally, but I never paid it too much attention. When I first moved to Phoenix, I had an encounter with a Bark Scorpion. It was crawling on the carpet in my living room, stopping a few inches from my tempting toes before I slammed a Tupperware container over it. I've even had Black Widow Spiders in my garage when I lived in California. But this was the first time I've had a giant spider like this here in Florida. It still gives me flashbacks.

If you've seen the movie "Arachnophobia," you may remember the spiders pouring from the toilet bowl, between the porcelain and the seat. After this incident, I can't get this image out of my head. Every time I use the facilities I do so with a certain amount of trepidation; I have to check and double-check the area before I begin.

I have not yet learned where the spider came from. How did it get into the bathroom? Maybe it moved in, pulling a little trailer with its belongings. But I hope it didn't bring its family with it.

If I've learned anything from this, it's that men should always pee standing up!

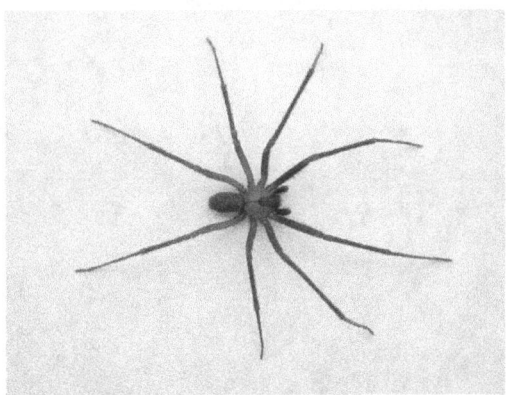

Brown Recluse Spider
(Actual size approx. 4" across to end of legs)

# # #

LIFE ON THE EDGE

September 2009

Tofino

The city of Tofino is located on the west coast of Vancouver Island, which itself is on the far west coast of Canada. Tofino is literally perched on the edge of the continent. There is an unobstructed view looking west across the open Pacific ocean from Tofino all the way to Japan.

The people in Tofino remind me of the characters from the book "The End of the Road," which is about the characters who decide to live in Alaska. Tofino residents share some of the same characteristics of all those who choose to make the west coast their home – except the folks in Tofino take it to an extreme.

The weather in Tofino is usually 10 degrees cooler than elsewhere on Vancouver Island (such as Victoria far to the south and east). And it's always cloudy. And rainy. I've been to Tofino many times in the past, and it always feels gloomy, no matter the season. This summer was no different. I was there in July when a record-breaking heat wave was blanketed the Pacific Northwest, with bright sunshine and low humidity. (Seattle hit 101F, the highest temperature ever there.) In Tofino, it was a cloudy 65F.

Tofino is full of tourists, mainly from Europe. It's a long way to go to get away from it all, but the surrounding area truly is "Super, Natural." The ocean is full of life, such as fish (salmon), whales (gray and orca (killer whales)), and surfers. Yes, surfers. The waves that strike the Tofino area beaches are much larger than elsewhere on the west coast, in part because of the unobstructed Pacific Ocean. The water is frigid (50F), so the surfers usually wear wet suits.

Many sportsmen choose to head into the forests and mountains for hunting. Nature enthusiasts head towards the Pacific Rim National Park for week long hikes. And bird lovers take guided tours to see wading birds, jays and other members of the crow family, and bald eagles that seem to be everywhere. The eagles are a magnificent sight. I was fortunate to see one swoop down and grab a fish from the harbor and fly away with it. The locals don't even bat an eye at these sights anymore.

Ucluelet

Heading straight south from Tofino one arrives at the only other city on the west coast of northern Vancouver Island: Ucluelet. The drive takes about an hour. During the trip I noticed signs advertising the "Edge-to-Edge" marathon that was taking place between Tofino and Ucluelet the next weekend. Those are hardy folk indeed.

Ucluelet used to be a small, sleepy fishing village, mainly populated by First Nations (Indians, Native Americans). I was last in Ucluelet in March 1987, when I went for a naughty weekend and to experience whale watching. The weekend was fun, but the whale watching was not: everyone on the boat became very ill, myself included. A word of warning: don't have a big fry-up breakfast before you head out on a 20-foot boat on rough seas to go whale watching. You'll spend most of your time doing other things instead.

This summer I found the same old ship hotel moored in the Ucluelet harbor. It looked the same as I remember it. But the surrounding area had changed quite a bit. The sleepy town was now bustling with tourists (this time from Vancouver, not Europe) and large new home developments were everywhere. Here in Florida, the real estate market has taken a beating recently. On Vancouver Island, the housing market is still booming. Modern condos were selling for over $650K – and these are in Ucluelet! It took me 3 hours to drive across the island from Parksville to Ucluelet. It's not exactly a metropolis offering modern conveniences. But maybe that's what makes it attractive.

I had a pleasant lunch in a small diner on Ucluelet's main street (one block long). On the way home I picked up a box of smoked salmon. It made a nice treat for breakfast the next day.

# # #

CALL AAA

October 2009

Welcome Home

I had returned earlier in the day from my summer travels. I had been away for nearly 2.5 months, visiting various parts of the US and Canada. When I finally got home, I was curious what would greet me inside the house. Memories of the "Buick in the Bathroom" were very fresh in my mind.

Fortunately, everything inside was fine. No significant water damage, no major insect population, no major anything. This was surprising, but welcome, news.

Unfortunately, everything outside was not so fine. In particular, my car would not start. I guess several months of sitting idle in the Florida heat had not been kind to it. The tires were OK. There was some sun damage to the paint. But the biggest problem was the battery: it was nearly dead. Since I had to go out to get some groceries, I called AAA.

Call AAA

I've been a member of AAA for over ten years. But I couldn't locate my membership card. Thankfully I had my membership information stored on my computer and online. I called AAA, verified that a call out and likely jump-start was free (included with the membership), and waited for them to arrive.

Maybe 20 minutes later the AAA guy called, asking for directions. It was a dark and stormy night. Really! Florida roads are so dark – you forget how dark they are until you see how bright the roads are in other parts of the country. Why don't we have streetlights here? The driver was close by, and he arrived in a few minutes.

I was waiting for him near the car. Just as he pulled up, it started to rain. Naturally. He verified that the battery was OK, just out of charge. I thought he'd bring out the jumper cables, but it seems I'm behind the times: they have a small portable device they use now. No need to put the cars nose-to-nose, no need to run long cables, no need to wonder which cable is hot and which is ground. Actually, you still need to know that; the sparks that resulted when he attached the cables the wrong way the first time attested to this.

Once the power was connected, the car started right away. He told me to keep it running for at least 20 minutes. I thanked him, and he walked back to his truck.

I was standing near my idling car, under my umbrella, making sure it didn't stall. A minute later the AAA guy came back, looking rather sheepish. "Can I borrow your phone?" he asked. His voice dropped a bit. "I need to call AAA. I locked my keys in the truck."

Call AAA ... Again

I was speechless. The irony of the AAA guy needing to call the AAA was not lost on me. But I also felt sorry for him: I knew he'd take quite a ribbing from his co-workers when they arrived. And I was right.

We stood under the small umbrella, both half-wet and half-dry as the rain continued to pour down. We chatted a bit about the sorts of calls he makes. In about 10 minutes the AAA called, asking for directions ... it seems the roads were still dark. ☺

When the second AAA truck arrived, two burly guys jumped out, looked at their hapless co-worker, and burst out laughing. While one of them took out the fish to pry open the window to get the lock open, the other kept up a steady stream of comments about how this would be talk of the garage for a while to come, how they had never heard of the AAA being called by the AAA, and wondering how much it would be worth to keep the matter quiet.

When the door was popped open, the driver hopped in the truck and drove away. I just looked at the other two guys and smiled. They were soaked from the rain but seemed happy. I guess this call was the highlight of their day. After a long day of travel, it was the highlight of mine too.

# # #

The Fob, the Key, and the Two PhDs

February 2010

Brrrr…

"Start, darn it!" For about the sixth time I turned the key. For about the sixth time the only result a slight clicking sound – then nothing. Definitely not the roar of the engine starting. I was at a loss. My aunt was going to be coming out soon; I was there to help her in a time of need, and I couldn't even manage the simplest of chauffeur duties?

My cousin might know what was wrong, but he was still at the hospital with his dad, so I couldn't call him. Besides, he hadn't used the car recently either: he has lived in a more temperate climate for many years now and was uncomfortable driving in the snow, and with the additional stress of the situation he had been taking cabs.

After a few more useless attempts to get the car started by myself, I decided to call my other cousin's husband. The first thing he asked me was, "Did you check the fob?" I thought I misunderstood the question. Or that maybe he was swearing at me for calling him so early in the morning. "The what?" I asked. "The fob," he said. "Is the light blinking?" When I said "no," he quickly replied, "Ah, that's the problem. The fob is not working."

I sat there pondering the situation. He was still on the phone, but I could tell he wanted to get back to bed. I just wanted to get going. I was freezing. I had arrived from Florida the night before, where it was 72 degrees. This morning it was -16F, a difference of 88 degrees – in the wrong direction. I had no hat, no gloves, and no boots. Since the car wouldn't start, there was no heat inside; the garage felt like an icebox. My teeth began to chatter.

I decided my next question should be simple and direct: "What the hell is a fob?"

The Fob

Winnipeg is the car theft capital of Canada. I doubt there are many "chop shops" in the city; who wants car parts that are frozen, rusted away from years of salt, and generally in poor condition? It seems teenagers looking for joy rides steal the vast majority of the cars. These thieves are quite brazen: cars are often stolen from house garages while people are asleep inside. The problem became so severe that the Manitoba DMV mandated the use of "the fob."

The "fob" is really just half of what is more properly called "the immobilizer." Although it sounds more like a scary wrestler, an immobilizer is an electronic device is installed behind the car's dashboard. Its circuitry sits between the ignition switch and the engine. A small red light on the dash blinks when it's ready: if the light is off, the car won't start.

The fob itself is a small piece of plastic, like a USB stick, that is put on the keychain. The fob interacts with the electronics behind the dash; they are paired so that one fob only works with one car. If you don't have the fob on your keychain and held near the dashboard, your car won't start.

In theory, this is a great solution. No one can steal your car without the fob (unless they know how to hack the device – which some do). In practice, there are some problems. For example, what if you don't have the fob on the keychain? More commonly, what happens when the fob doesn't communicate with the rest of the immobilizer's electronics behind the dashboard? The car won't start.

When would technology ever fail? The answer is … quite often – when it's -40F degree weather that lasts for days (and sometimes weeks) at a time. Do you ever read the back of devices like radios for "normal operating temperature range"? That morning I felt like I was out of that range. And again, on the wrong side: this was Winterpeg, not Phoenix.

Bless This Fob

My other cousin's husband as right: the problem was the fob. But how to fix it? The solution was simple: "Wave it around a little bit," he said. "When the light goes on, just turn the key." Simple to say; difficult to do. The fob seemed to have a mind of its own. Sometimes it would "talk" to the rest of the immobilizer and decide it was OK for the car to start. Other times it would turn off the light while I was turning the key, just before ignition. I think it was just being belligerent.

I have a Ph.D. in computer science. My cousin has a Ph.D. in physics. People sometimes refer to a Ph.D. as "piled higher and deeper" – and they're not referring to knowledge. That was the case here: little good all this education did us in this situation. All I could do was wave the silly fob around in front of the dashboard, hoping the immobilizer would recognize it and let the car start. I felt helpless.

The problem persisted during the entirety of my visit, but the malicious fob ended up providing a little bit of levity for my cousin and me during a difficult time. Whenever I went to the car, I mentally prepared myself with threats, prayers, and improvised holy water (which was melted snow dripping from my cold hands). "Bless this fob and all those who ride in this car." Sometimes it worked. Mostly I just warmed myself up with some energetic cursing and kept trying to start the car until the fob decided to give in. Sometimes that worked too.

By the time I left to return to Florida, I wished some thieves would come along and steal the car. At least then I could get a fob-free rental to use.

# # #

Goodbye, Uncle Kirk

February 2010

I had gone to Winnipeg during the coldest part of the winter to help my cousin deal with his mother and his dying father. His father, my Uncle Kirk, was in palliative care due to cancer. The chemo and radiation therapies had run their course. It was only a matter of days before he passed away.

When I first saw my uncle, I could hardly recognize him. He was small, thin, and very frail looking. He was lying in a hospital bed, barely conscious. His hair was unkempt, he was unshaven, and his dentures had been removed. But when I clutched his hand and said I was there, he moved a bit and mumbled a few words that I hoped meant he knew I was there with him.

The change in his appearance reminded me of a time just a few years earlier. My neighbor had cancer, and I had not seen him in quite a while. When I went over to his house to visit, he was sitting on the sofa with his wife. She looked much the same, but I truly couldn't recognize him. He was more than thin – he was gaunt. Cancer does terrible things to people.

My cousin's sister, her husband, and their children did visit the hospital to see my uncle, but only once that I can remember. The children were teenagers, and the whole experience was too intense for them. This meant I spent a lot of time in the palliative care ward in the hospital, swapping shifts with my cousin and his mother. It's hard to stay positive in such an environment. The people there are not just sick, they are dying. It's the last stop before the hereafter and everyone knows it. Hope is gone.

Over the next few days, I sat in the room with my uncle. He was non-responsive most of the time. I couldn't help thinking back to the time when he was such a vibrant and healthy man, full of the joys of life. I looked in on their home in Fort Pierce, Florida during the 2004/2005 hurricanes. He was so concerned about the roofing; now those concerns seemed pointless. There was a time when he had to cut back on cheese and wine due to high cholesterol; now I couldn't help feeling that such deprivations are a waste of time. Life is meant to be lived.

I was with my uncle when he passed. It was one of the most unforgettable experiences of my life. Here one minute, gone the next. But at least it was peaceful; no more intermittent moaning that sounded so dreadful and heartrending.

My parents have been dealing with dying friends for years. It comes with getting old I suppose. But this was the first time I've experienced death in the family firsthand since my grandfathers died in 1976, and my grandmother passed away in 1993. It doesn't make me look forward to that aspect of my own future.

My aunt was sitting in a chair in front of the bed with my cousin when my uncle passed. She had lost her partner of 60 years. She never really recovered from the loss. Within six months of his passing, she was incapable of living alone. She quickly lost most of her faculties and slipped away from us into her own world.

After the doctors had completed their work, my cousin took my aunt out of the room. I started to collect my uncle's belongings: his comb, a few clothes, his glasses. It was depressing to realize that when you shuffle off the mortal coil, all your worldly possessions can be held in a Ziploc bag.

Standing alone in his room, I quietly said, "Goodbye, Uncle Kirk" one last time, and walked out. I returned home to Florida the next day.

# # #

SICK IN THE CITY OF LIGHT

April 2010

Images of Paris

Think of Paris. What images pop into your head? The Eiffel Tower? The Louvre Museum? The Notre-Dame Cathedral? People lounging in cafes along the Champs-Élysées? Beautiful women walking their poodles into jewelry stores? All of these are indeed present.

But Paris (and France in general) is also well known for its fabulous food. There are fancy shops selling decadent pastries, seafood stalls selling their fresh (aka smelly) oysters on the sidewalk, and restaurants offering rare meals such as "steak tartare." It's all available for your gastronomic delight.

But there's a darker side to the food in the "City of Light": it can make you sick.

Conference Food

I was in Paris for a conference. The event was held at a university in the 13th arrondissement (administrative district), somewhat removed from the city center. All of our meals were held in the student cafeteria. I've eaten in student cafeterias around the world, and for the most part, I can say that the food there is the same. That is, the food is terrible.

The food in the Paris student cafeteria was no different. Rubber chick, raw veal, and undercooked fish were the main dishes of the day. The only items on offer that were tasty were the desserts: cheese and wine. Yes, they serve wine in the student cafeteria. They serve wine everywhere in Paris. It's cheap, and it's excellent. I learned long ago to imbibe while traveling – it helps kill the local bugs.

Friday is fish day, and that's what I had for lunch. I was so busy talking during the meal that I almost didn't notice that the fish was basically uncooked. By that time it was too late. All I could do was hope the sauce (and the wine) would help.

Dinner in the Latin Quarter

The next day the conference was over. A bunch of us decided to go to the Latin Quarter, which is perhaps the most "touristy" of locations in Paris. I visited the magnificent Notre-Dame Cathedral and then strolled into the restaurant area across the Seine. I should have taken the opportunity to pray.

The Latin Quarter is densely packed, with narrow streets and wide people. The restaurants all have hosts standing in their doorways, beckoning you to enter. We chose a Greek place and went inside.

I should have known there were going to be problems when my meal arrived and it was the wrong order. I sent it back, and in a few short minutes, the lamb I had ordered arrived. I think I could still hear it bleating: it was basically raw. I sent it back and waited again. It came back in a few minutes, a little more burnt on the outside. A quick cut revealed a rare center. I thought about sending it back again, but arguing with a loud Greek maître d' in broken French (his, not mine) was becoming tiresome. I decided to throw in the towel; I nibbled only at the edges.

The Trip Home

I was scheduled to return home on Sunday. The flight was leaving CDG at 1:30 pm, which meant I had to be at the airport by 11:00 am or so. At 4:00 am I was already awake – sitting in the "library" with "stomach problems." Why did it have to be the travel day? The trip from Paris to Florida was going to take me about 16 hours, and doing it while sick was not a pleasant prospect.

I always carry certain medicine when I travel abroad. One of the most important is the pink pills we're all familiar with. However, I had very little time before I had to leave the hotel, and I could not afford to be searching for facilities every few minutes, so in this case, I needed the nuclear version: Imodium. Think of it like a chemical cork.

Did I mention that the French trains were on strike? And that the French subways have no elevators or escalators? Carrying luggage up and down many flights of stairs in the Paris subway system is never fun at the best of times. I doubted I could do it now. Fortunately, I was able to hire a driver to take me directly from the hotel to the airport for €55.

I made it to the airport, looking green and feeling worse. When I got to the Delta check-in area, I was told that the flight to Atlanta was over-sold. "Would I like to volunteer to stay an extra night in Paris? $1000, free hotel, and food vouchers." I said "yes" right away, thinking that the extra day of rest would help settle my system. The people in the Air France lounge were very kind, giving me a place to rest. Unfortunately, by the time I got to the gate the airline no longer needed volunteers. So I boarded the plane for the 11-hour flight home: 9½ hours in the air, and 1½ sitting on the tarmac.

I made it to Atlanta without incident. I went through customs and immigration, re-checked my bags, and sought the nearest Delta lounge. About five minutes after sitting down in the lounge I had to do an "O.J. Simpson" to the nearest restroom. I was sick as a dog for the next 20 minutes. All the time I was cursing everything French.

Recovery

After I finally got home, it took me about three days to recover. Travel is tiring. There's a six-hour time change between here and Paris. And traveling while sick really takes it out of you (literally and figuratively).

If there was any silver lining in this episode, it was that I left Paris a week before the ash from the erupting volcano in Iceland closed the major airports in Europe for nearly a week – including CDG. If I had been forced to spend several days "camping" in the airport while being sick, I don't know how I would have coped. I carry extra insulin and needles, but I would have run out in two days.

And I would still be eating French food. Airport food. Yech.

# # #

The Vicious Swans

June 2010

Outrunning the Competition

They say if you run in a zigzag manner you can outrun an alligator. I don't know if it's true or if it's an old wives' tale. But since moving to Florida, I've never had to test the theory.

They also say if you run as fast as you can you can't outrun a bear. And climbing a tree doesn't always work. Thankfully I've never had to test these theories either.

I prefer the axiom that you don't need to outrun the alligators or the bears – you only need to outrun the competition. The animals will get the laggards while you make your escape. It might be cowardly, but at least you get to survive and embellish the tale later.

A Day at the Park

I was visiting Pittsburgh for the first time in several years since I had moved to California. It was a beautiful Fall day. The crispness in the air, the color of the leaves, the smell of wood smoke in the air – all made me want to go for a walk in beautiful North Park (which is close to where I used to live). As the afternoon wore on, I decided to drive to the park.

One of the many attractions in North Park is the lakes that dot the landscape. If you're active, you can go kayaking, swimming (when the water's not too polluted), or fishing. If you just want to relax, beautiful forests and fields, with picnic tables and large gazebos suitable for family outings, surround the lakes.

The park is full of wildlife. As with most of Pittsburgh, there are deer everywhere – especially at dawn and at dusk. There is also the usual collection of smaller animals, such as raccoons and skunks that lurk in the bush, just waiting for the people to leave.

Attack!

I parked in one of the main lots and headed for the lake near the center of the park. Many years ago I used to sit near the water's edge and watch the ducks and geese. I thought I'd see if anything had changed since my last visit.

When I was about five feet from the lake I was startled by a loud honking sound and wild flapping noises. All I could see where giant white wings looming over me, a large beak – no, two beaks! -- lunging towards my head, with feathers flying everywhere. I was frozen with surprise and (I'll admit it) fear. I was under attack!

I decided to test the theory of outrunning the competition. But in this case I was alone – there was no competition. I quickly wondered what the rules were for outrunning swans. That's right: two vicious swans were chasing me!

These weren't the swans you see swimming languidly along a river in Oxford, looking elegant and majestic. There were nasty, vicious beasts, 10 feet tall, with gnashing teeth, razor sharp claws, and a bad attitude. At least that's what I saw when I turned over my shoulder while running away from the lake.

If I knew how things were going to turn out, I would have contacted the folks from "When Animals Attack" before I went to the park. A grown man, flapping his arms, running away from swans flapping their wings – and neither party getting airborne. If I was going to look like a fool, I should have been paid for it.

It seems I had stumbled into the swan's nest, and they were rather protective of their young signets. How was I to know they had chosen this part of this lake in North Park for a home? I was looking for cute little ducks, not giant vicious swans.

* * *

For the record, I still don't know if running in a zigzag pattern is better than running in a straight line to get away from ferocious fowl. I was running like the proverbial chicken with no head, and I don't know what pattern they follow before expiring. But I know how my run ended: collapsing on the ground near my car, gasping for breath, and hoping no lurking skunk decided to take advantage of the situation.

# # #

Immortality Chardonnay

September 2010

Recaş Vineyards

It should have been a dark and stormy night. But it wasn't; it was a sunny and bright afternoon. We were on a tour of the Recaş Vineyards, located in the Banat region of Romania. In the middle of a fairly typical Eastern European city is this oasis of rolling hills, quiet gardens, and rows and rows of beautiful grapes. I went there expecting a "Transylvania" atmosphere; what I found was the Napa Valley of Eastern Europe.

The tour included a 7-course wine tasting experience. A variety of wines were sampled: white, red, rose, desert, even mead (I know that's not technically a wine). All the wine bottles did have "Transylvania" stamped on the back, which gave them a little bit of exotic feeling. The most impressive label I found was a bottle that had "Immortality Chardonnay" written across the front in a suitably gothic font.

I was looking for a nice "Vlad the Impaler" Cabernet, but for some reason, it was never on the menu. At a restaurant the previous night a friend asked the waitress, "Can I drink this red wine? I'm a vegetarian." Her only response was a cold stare. It might have been a "lost in translation" issue, but I think it more likely that they've heard all the vampire jokes before.

Poe's Crows

If you've read Edger Allen Poe, you know how the crow is a symbol of death, a harbinger of bad things to come. Native Americans use the crow in funeral ceremonies. Some people think having a crow land on your windowsill is a sign of back luck.

So it should be no surprise that the predominant bird I encountered in Transylvania was the crow. There were murders of them perched in the trees across from the hotel every night, squawking and flapping around, occasionally dive-bombing pedestrians.

I wondered if these were "vampire crows," the type that doesn't just peck at your head but sucks your blood if they can. Who wants to feel their sharp beaks and black tongues on your neck? I decided to walk on the other side of the street, just to be safe. Why take a chance?

Twilight Mosquitos

Actually, the bloodsuckers in Transylvania were the mosquitos. I was surprised to find them visiting my room every night. I was not in Florida, where mosquitoes are omnipresent. Why were there so many of them in Romania?

Then I started to worry about getting bitten by these tiny vampires. Forget about West Nile Virus; these fanged insects probably carried the Twilight Virus. I spent half my time in bed swatting them away, wondering if I should avoid the sun the next morning – just in case I had been bitten during the night.

Interestingly, there were a lot of bats flying around outside. I was not keen on inviting any of them into my room though. Maybe they were more interested in traditional vampire fare than normal bat food – man over mosquito.

In the end, on most evenings I decided to try another sip of the Immortality Chardonnay – purely for medicinal purposes of course.

# # #

SNOW TIRES

December 2010

During a recent visit to Montreal, my dad had to take his car to the garage. Every Fall the ritual of putting on the snow tires takes place. A few years ago, the Quebec government mandated the use of "real" snow tires, as opposed to the all-season radials that everyone had been using for years.

This was a "back to the future" moment, since in the past people were used to changing tires every Fall and Spring. But the ritual was thankfully retired when new all-season tires came out. It seems the tires were not quite good enough for the harsh Canadian winters. Either that or the government was in cahoots with the tire and garage industry.

The forced tire change involves an extra expense for all drivers. But it's good business for garages, since they will store your unused tires between seasons for a sizable fee. Tires are tremendously heavy, which means few people are willing to lug the summer/winter tires down the stairs to store them in their basement. Storing them outside is not really an option because the Montreal winters are so cold the tires would freeze and crack.

Where are the Hubcaps?

I took my dad's car out to the store to run some errands. When I was walking back to the car in the parking lot I noticed something looked different. The tires had no hubcaps. I looked around and saw that most of the other cars also lacked hubcaps.

Car owners in Montreal usually get their winter tires from discount stores. After all, they have to pay for two sets of tires: summer and winter. This means the hubcaps rarely match the two sets of tires. In the winter, the tires go bare. Very few people are willing to buy a second set of hubcaps.

The owners who get their snow tires from the dealer can choose to match the summer tires. Everyone can tell who forked over the extra money for matching tires by identifying the cars with hubcaps still on in the winter.

Most people opt for the hubcap-less look. All winter you see cars driving around that look like they've been the victims of petty theft. It's not pretty – but then, neither is winter.

# # #

STINK BUGS

January 2011

What is that smell?

Living in Florida, I am used to bugs. Ants, roaches, even gecko lizards have roamed my house at various times. During the summer I have the pest control people on speed dial.

When I arrived in Pittsburgh in October, bugs were the last things on my mind. The weather was already turning cool. A few caterpillars were still in the trees, but the robins were gone, so most of the insects should have been gone by this time of year too.

A few days after I settled into my new place, I noticed several bugs crawling up the walls. They were not moving very fast; some seemed to stay in one place for a long time. I used some tissue from the bathroom to grab one of the bugs, half squishing it as I did so. The result was a terrible stench that made me feel dizzy. What was that smell?

Arrival

I lived in Pittsburgh before: from 1995-1998 I learned about hoagies, terrible towels, and what it means to "bleed black & gold." But after three years I grew tired of the cold damp weather and the unremitting gloominess. There is more sunshine in Seattle than there is in Pittsburgh. I decamped for Southern California in the winter of 1998 and never looked back. But as the saying goes, "never say never." I had planned on spending part of my sabbatical at NASA's JPL with CalTech in Pasadena, but the government's cuts to the space program eliminated the funding for visiting faculty. So Pittsburgh and Carnegie Mellon University it was.

Pittsburgh's population doesn't change very much: for everyone who leaves, someone else arrives. As I was leaving western Pennsylvania in 1998, a newcomer was arriving in eastern Pennsylvania. But the newcomer was unwelcome, and it has become the scourge of the Mid-Atlantic States: the Brown Marmorated Stink Bug. It looks like a potato bug on steroids.

In 1998, in Allentown (PA), a stink bug was found in a container from Asia. They're agricultural pests in China, Korea, and Taiwan, but they've become more than that to me: they've become my obsession.

It's War!

I don't mind bugs too much. As I said, I'm used to roaches. I do draw the line at large spiders though (cf. "The Buick in the Bathroom"). But stink bugs are different. They are hardy, they are everywhere, and they won't go away.

I threw one into the fireplace, with the fire on, only to see it crawl out a few minutes later. I did this twice and it still kept coming, like some insect version of Freddy Kruger.

I've frozen stink bugs. They do die this way, but it takes a long time. If you remove them from the freezer before a few hours have passed, they lie dormant for a while then they revive and start moving around again, like some creepy-crawly Energizer Bunny. Until now I'd only seen scorpions do this in the desert.

They have no natural enemies. They are too big for Pittsburgh's spiders to catch, and the birds don't seem attracted to them. The only fowl that will eat them are chickens – and that's when the chickens are fed the bugs by the bucketful by weary farmers.

When the temperature climbs over 45F, the bugs start appearing in the house. But I never see them entering into the room; they just "appear" on the walls. Maybe they have a miniature Star Trek transporter system they brought with them. I've found them on my clothes – which is rather unnerving and which has made me as paranoid as a cowboy checking his boots. I've stepped on them in the shower – without my glasses, I didn't know what I had touched, but my nose knew soon enough. They've landed on my arms while I'm asleep. (Did I mention that they fly too?)

The last straw was seeing two of them crawling on my toothbrush. That was it. It was war, man versus bug, and I was in it to win.

BugZooka

I looked online, even checking Wikipedia (cf. today's article in Florida Today), trying to find a way to defeat the stink bugs. It seemed many people were fighting the same battle. Some had what I can only describe as an infestation: hundreds of the bugs climbing the outside walls and entering the house. The local newspaper ran a story with exasperated people saying, "I'd rather have chicken shit all over the place than these stink bugs." Pest control experts say there is very little that can be done to control them.

Some people said to freeze them; as I said, I tried that. Some people recommended putting them in a dish of warm water with Dawn dishwashing liquid; the soap masks their smell. But you still need to get them from the wall to the soap dish. I decided to try a more aggressive solution: I ordered the BugZooka.

The BugZooka is a vacuum-powered bug collector. It has a long attachment that can reach to the ceiling. The bugs are sucked into the top of the tube and remain there. You can watch them ("Hey kids, come see the bugs!"), release them humanely (hah!), or leave them until they die. I admit that, as an experiment, I did the latter; I can report the bugs last two nasty days before expiring.

Now I roam the house with the BugZooka in hand. Whenever I enter a room, I scan the walls looking for stink bugs. I won't put on clothes without examining them and shaking them off. I won't brush my teeth or comb my hair without checking everything first. But I feel a sense of accomplishment when I hear the satisfying "thunk" of the bug gun working its magic. And there is no stink.

* * *

PS: I was at the Pittsburgh Filmmakers School last week. During class we had to stop to kill stink bugs that were flying into the lights, landing in peoples' hair, and crawling everywhere. I wished I had my trusty BugZooka with me.

Then I realized the stink bug story would make a great screenplay for a movie. Maybe Peter Billingsley will play me. You'll shoot your eye out...

# # #

Are Big Words Good?

March 2011

See Dick. See Dick run.

When we first learn to write, we use small words to create simple sentences. *See Dick. See Dick run. See Jane.* As we gain mastery of syntax and grammar, we write in a more sophisticated manner. But does sophisticated always have to mean more? Does it have to mean using words that are so uncommon that the reader must reach for their dictionary to understand the sentence?

Some writers maintain and even perfect a minimalist style. Michael Crichton's books read very much like a screenplay. The story is plot-driven and moves along very fast.

Other writers, particularly essayists and columnists, seem to excel in their use of extravagant vocabulary. William F. Buckley, Jr. is a good example of this type of writer. He appeared to take pleasure in lifting his conversation over the heads of some of the people he interviewed on television.

In a recent column in *Florida Today* titled "The Case for Brevity," Al Neuharth wrote the following:

Getting things short and to the point is the most important thing we should keep in mind in our personal or professional lives. In writing or speaking. From grade school to high school to college to our job.

Personally, I like to see authors extend themselves – and challenge their readers – with a masterful display of the English language. But some writers can go too far. If they use a thesaurus as often as they use a mouse when writing, something is amiss. Why use arcane words when modern ones would suffice? And what does "arcane" mean?

Writing Exercise

As part of a screenwriting class, I had an exercise recently that focused on simplicity. I had to write a scene where no sentence was more than five words line, and (with a few exceptions) no word could be more than two syllables. Being forced to write in such a style makes you focus on what you want to say. All the detritus, err, extraneous, err, extra words must be removed.

Eschew Obfuscation

Below is a list of some unusual words that are used several times in a book I recently finished reading. Do you know what they mean? Can you use them in a sentence? Can you think of a better synonym that could be used instead?

Puissant: –adjective, Literary. powerful; mighty; potent.

Roborant: –adjective, strengthening. –noun, a tonic.

Theurgy: –noun, plural -gies.1. a system of beneficent magic practiced by the Egyptian Platonists and others. 2. the working of a divine or supernatural agency in human affairs.

Clinquant: –adjective, 1. glittering, especially with tinsel; decked with garish finery. –noun, 2. imitation gold leaf; tinsel; false glitter.

Nacre: –noun, mother-of-pearl. [–noun, 1. a hard, iridescent substance that forms the inner layer of certain mollusk shells, used for making buttons, beads, etc.; nacre.]

Eldritch: –adjective, eerie; weird; spooky.

Ineffable: –adjective, 1. incapable of being expressed or described in words; inexpressible: ineffable joy. 2. not to be spoken because of its sacredness; unutterable: the ineffable name of the deity.

Solipsism: –noun, 1. Philosophy. the theory that only the self exists, or can be proved to exist. 2. extreme preoccupation with and indulgence of one's feelings, desires, etc.; egoistic self-absorption.

Destrier: —noun Archaic . a war-horse; charger.

Illimitable: —adjective, not limitable; limitless; boundless.

Munificent: —adjective, 1. extremely liberal in giving; very generous. 2. characterized by great generosity: a munificent bequest.

Verdure: —noun, 1. greenness, especially of fresh, flourishing vegetation. 2. green vegetation, especially grass or herbage. 3. freshness in general; flourishing condition; vigor.

Sapid: —adjective, 1. having taste or flavor. 2. agreeable to the taste; palatable. 3. agreeable, as to the mind; to one's liking.

Transubstantiation: —noun, 1. the changing of one substance into another. 2. Theology. the changing of the elements of the bread and wine, when they are consecrated in the Eucharist, into the body and blood of Christ (a doctrine of the Roman Catholic Church).

Orogeny: —noun, Geology. the process of mountain making or upheaval.

Lambent: —adjective, 1. running or moving lightly over a surface: lambent tongues of flame. 2. dealing lightly and gracefully with a subject; brilliantly playful: lambent wit. 3. softly bright or radiant: a lambent light.

Redolent: —adjective, 1. having a pleasant odor; fragrant. 2. odorous or smelling (usually followed by of): redolent of garlic. 3. suggestive; reminiscent (usually followed by of): verse redolent of Shakespeare.

Bedizen: —verb (used with object), to dress or adorn in a showy, gaudy, or tasteless manner.

Sendaline: -noun, a type of thin silk cloth.

Threnody: —noun, plural -dies. a poem, speech, or song of lamentation, especially for the dead; dirge; funeral song.

Many of these words have their origins in the middle ages, ancient Celtic tales, or in religion. Thank goodness for devices like the Kindle, which have a thesaurus just a click away. Otherwise, one needs a puissant and sapid roborant for the illimitable headaches that bring ineffable pain and are sure to follow.

# # #

CLEARING THE CAR

June 2011

It was another return trip from Florida to Pittsburgh. I rarely arrived in a good mood on these trips, particularly at this time of the year. By early December the weather was turning terrible in southwestern Pennsylvania. During the plane's approach to the airport, I could see the bleak landscape out the window. The sky was leaden, the trees were bare, and there was snow on the ground. Compared to the warm sun and lush greenery that I had left a few hours ago, this was a depressing sight. I wondered again how people could live in such a setting … until I remembered that I was living there now too.

My car was parked in the long-term lot. As soon as I got outside of the terminal, I felt a blast of cold air. My thin suit jacket was of little comfort against the 22F weather. I hurried as best I could, dragging my luggage over the icy ruts and through the snowdrifts on the road. When I got to my car I groaned: it was covered in a foot of snow.

When I left Pittsburgh a few weeks earlier, I had not yet purchased a scraper. I had to be creative. I managed to sweep a bit of snow off of the trunk with my arm. I then used a straw beach mat that was in the trunk to remove the snow from the car.

I must have looked very comical, sweeping a wobbly rolled-up mat to move the snow from the car, cursing while I worked. Swearing is like shivering: it helps keeps your body warm. People in Pittsburgh just think you're angry over the latest Steeler's football game.

Eventually, the car was mostly cleared of snow. But now it was covered in straw, as if it had been parked in a wind-blown barn. I wondered what people would think when they saw straw flying off the car on the highway when everyone else had snow swirling off theirs. Maybe the Florida license plates would explain things.

There was one last challenge: the door lock was frozen. There must have been freezing rain before the first snowstorm, so there was a layer of ice under the snow. Anyone who grew up in a northern climate knows there's a natural (but nasty) way to de-ice a car lock. But it's not fun to do in the cold. Fortunately, I didn't have to resort to such extreme measures. I had a cup of coffee with me, and it was still warm enough to do the job. But now the car door was covered in coffee-colored straw.

Fortunately, the car started. The wheels were slightly egg-shaped from being frozen in place, but once on the road they eventually returned to form. I decided to stop at Wal-Mart on the way home to buy a proper ice scraper and snow sweeper. They were sold out. I tried Home Depot, Target, and Giant Eagle (a grocery store), but the result was always the same. This didn't improve my mood. The only consolation was that this time next year I would be using the straw mat to lay on the beach, while people here would still be clearing their car.

###

LIVING WELL WITH DIABETES

August 2011

I was diagnosed with Type 1 (insulin dependent) diabetes in 1993. Since then I've struggled to manage this chronic condition on a daily basis. But I've also learned how to live as best I can while dealing with the inevitable problems that affect diabetic men as they age. My first challenge was learning more about insulin. The rest of my challenges mainly centered on the inevitable side effects that manifest themselves over the years, such as high blood pressure.

Insulin is a hormone that regulates the amount of glucose in the blood. In a healthy person, cells in the pancreas produce insulin. A Type I (previously called juvenile-onset) diabetic produces no insulin at all. A Type II diabetic (the more common type) produces some insulin, but their cells do not process it correctly.

Years ago, a diagnosis of diabetes meant nearly starving oneself to reduce glucose (sugar) in the body, and still, the outlook was grim. For example, children with Type I diabetes rarely lived more than a year after diagnosis. The prognosis improved after Banting & Macleod were awarded the Nobel Prize in Medicine in 1923 for their discovery of insulin, which they purified from the pancreas of a dog. Their breakthrough changed the lives of millions of diabetics for the better.

For many years, diabetics injected insulin extracted from the pancreas of pigs, since it was the closest to human insulin. Most people now use human biosynthetic insulin that is manufactured using recombinant DNA technology. This has improved treatment considerably.

Injections

For about the next 70 years, people with diabetes have been using syringes to give themselves daily injections. As an insulin-dependent diabetic myself, I've long been resigned to this fact. I'm glad that rDNA insulin exists because without it I'd literally be dead. But I never liked the needles very much.

I once decided to do a calculation of the number of injections I've given myself since I was first diagnosed in 1993 until 2011. The number of injections per day has increased from three during 1993-1995 to six now. The total number of needles I've given myself is approximately 30,660.

- 1993 – 1995: 3 / day

- 1996 – 2000: 4 / day

- 2001 – 2008: 5 / day

- 2009 – 2011 (half): 6 / day

TOTAL: $(365 * 3 * 3) + (365 * 5 * 4) + (365 * 8 * 5) + (365 * 2.5 * 6) = $ **30,660** .

A while ago someone asked me if the needles still hurt. Even after 30000 shots, they do.

More importantly, my tissue was becoming damaged from repeated injections. I rotate the injection sites as you are supposed to: upper arms, belly, legs. I don't do buttocks because it's too hard to do properly. (Contrary to what my students sometimes say, I don't have eyes in the back of my head.) I don't like doing my thighs because I usually hit muscle and it feels like an electric shock. Fortunately, my belly has ample padding.

However, even rotating the injection site doesn't prevent tissue damage over the long term. It causes the fatty tissue to thicken, creating lumps that you can feel. This effect is called lipodystrophy and leads to erratic absorption of the insulin from that site.

This was happening to me, causing my blood sugar readings to be wildly unpredictable. I could eat the same foods, and do the same activity, with a reading one day of 150 and a reading the next day of 280. My HA1C readings were also stuck north of 8.7. Something had to be done.

Insulin Pumps

There are many paths to living well with diabetes. Good control is essential. A healthy diet is important. Counting carbohydrates for every meal is essential. Exercise should be part of the overall plan. But in the end, for insulin-dependent diabetics, all roads lead to the pump.

An insulin pump is a device that uses a cannula (a small, flexible needle) for subcutaneous insertion and a plastic tube to connect the cannula to an insulin reservoir. The reservoir is part of a small device, typically worn on a belt, which holds the insulin and the control system for managing the actual delivery of insulin. People who use insulin pumps usually say their control of daily glucose levels improves – and it all but eliminates the need for multiple daily injections. The cannula is replaced every three days or so. Goodbye needles!

I always knew that the endgame would be the pump. But I was not keen on strapping myself with yet another device – particularly one that had loose tubing connecting the pump (hooked to your belt) to a cannula (a small, flexible needle) for subcutaneous insulin delivery. The tubes have to be disconnected for showers, swimming, and other forms of exercise. I worried about pulling out the cannula while I was asleep. I've heard stories of people's dogs grabbing the tubes in their mouths and running away, leaving their owners to watch in horror as the tube spools out until … yank … the needle was ripped out of the belly.

For those who mastered the pump, they swear by it; their daily blood glucose levels become much better. More importantly, their quarterly HA1C levels often drop below 7, which is a target for a Type I diabetic. I was 6.8 … once. I wanted to get back.

Fortunately, technology has come to my rescue. A new wireless insulin pump is on the market. It looks like a small computer mouse. It's worn directly on the injection site. It communicates with a PDA-like device that I use to monitor and control it. It's replaced every three days. No tubes, and no more needles!

I tried using this wireless insulin pump for a few weeks. Sadly, it kept failing at an alarming rate. The idea was good, but the production quality was poor. For a lifesaving device like an insulin pump, the failure rate was unacceptably high. I had to adopt a more conventional pump, tubes and all. But at least it works almost all of the time. And it really does work: my blood glucose levels have improved, and so has my quality of life. Now I could turn my attention to more pressing matters: testosterone.

Testosterone

I'm sure you're familiar with all those ED (erectile dysfunction) advertisements on TV. The camera shows a senior-ish couple relaxing in his-and-her bathtubs on a cliff, overlooking an ocean, holding hands, looking pleased with themselves. The implication is that the "event" has just occurred, or is about to occur. The ad's tagline is, "Be ready when the moment strikes." For the happy couple, all is right with the world – made possible through modern pharmaceuticals.

For diabetics, ED is usually caused by neuropathy (nerve damage). There are of course other reasons, such as fatigue due to constant high blood sugar, and psychological issues such as depression from dealing with a chronic disease like diabetes, but nerve damage is the leading physiological reason.

But what if you're younger than the happy couple in the ads? What if you don't (yet) have neuropathy "down there"? Are there other symptoms that you've been ignoring?

If you want your mojo back, you should check your testosterone level. Testosterone is an essential male hormone. It's not too much of an overstatement to say that it's a big part of what makes a man a man. Since Type I diabetes is an endocrine problem, hormones play an essential role in your overall health.

Low testosterone is not something that most doctors test for unless you ask. But you need to know what to look for. This is easy in retrospect but hard when the symptoms are discrete – but the pattern is only obvious when many of them are present. This is another example of how you need to take control of your own health to live well with diabetes.

One symptom is fatigue. But this is a common symptom for many conditions. In my case, I have other medical conditions besides diabetes, such as arthritis, which causes me to get very poor sleep. I'm chronically tired. It's been decades since I slept for more than four hours at a time. The lack of quality sleep causes widespread damage.

Another symptom is the unstated issue of the bathtub couple: challenges in the bedroom. I thought it was just regular slowdown due to my age. Or my chronic fatigue. But another reason is a lack of desire, which no number of pills will fix. And this lack of desire is a key indicator of low testosterone.

Increased belly fat is another sign of low testosterone. It also happens as we get older, but not always so much, so fast. It's due to cortisol buildup, which in turn is affected by testosterone. Honestly, I thought it was due to my recent infatuation with nighttime potato chips.

A more serious symptom for Type I diabetics is insulin resistance. This is something that was happening to me: my daily insulin requirement was increasing significantly.

Equally serious is osteoporosis. It turns out that low testosterone is the leading cause of osteoporosis in men my age. Osteoporosis is usually something older women suffer from; I've had it for five years, but in the last two years it's gotten a lot worse.

I decided to force my doctor to give me a testosterone test, which is just a blood test. A normal reading is between 800-1000. My test result was 210. A second test a month later was 200. That's low. Something had to be done.

Gel

The first line of treatment is a gel called Testim. It comes in small tubes. You apply it to your shoulder every morning or evening. I called it "spreading the love." It's a bit messy, but at least it's painless.

It comes with a warning not to let a woman touch your skin for several hours after you apply the gel. This rather defeats the reason for the gel, doesn't it?

After four months of Testim I felt ... the same. The blood test showed a testosterone level of 205. It was back to the drawing board.

Injections

The next line of treatment is injections. I called them "Cupid's Needles." They are usually given every two weeks. Most doctors require you go to into their office for the treatment, but I was out of town – and I'm used to giving myself insulin injections anyway – so they let me do it myself.

It hurts. The needle needs to go deep into the muscle. The hormone is held in a very viscous oil solution, so it's hard to pull into the syringe. It's even harder to inject into the arm. The needle is so fat that it feels like a railroad tie going into your flesh. It's actually supposed to go into your butt, but let's just say that's not always convenient.

I had numerous conversations at the Walgreen's window about needle gauge, needle length, syringe types, and so on. I have to say I didn't appreciate doing this in public. But eventually, I got the right combination of syringes, needles, and plungers.

The injections did work in the sense that I had more energy and my blood tests showed the testosterone levels had gone up – a lot – but the results are in waves. You go from sheep to stallion and back again. The bathtub couple would be on a roller coaster, not resting comfortably on a cliff looking over the ocean.

There's an old saying that the only way to hurt someone who's lost everything is to give them back something they once had – only broken. It's hyperbole to say that this is the case here, but having been the horse for a while, it's hard to go back to being the lamb.

I decided to try the last line of treatment: pellets.

Pellets

Sadly, they are not at all like the pellets you feed to a gerbil: these pellets require minor surgery to implant subcutaneously. I had read about other people's experiences with the pellets, which ranged from "excellent" to "avoid at all costs." Still, I wanted to get better, so I decided a visit to the urologist was in order.

A Visit to the Urologist

At this point, it's important to note that my endocrinologist prescribed the gel and the needle treatments. Obtaining the drugs and the necessary supplies only required a trip to the drugstore. Pellets are something else entirely. They required a trip to a part of the clinic I'd been able to avoid up until then: urology.

What do most men immediately think of when they hear the word "urologist"? Yes indeed, unwanted images of that "special exam," the "procedure that dares not speak its name," pop into your head.

I found the waiting room full of nervous looking men, most quite a bit older than me. No one was making eye contact. I guess everyone knew what was in store when they went through the doors.

I believe women are more used to (if not more comfortable with) similar situations related to their visits to the gynecologist. But things change when it's you in the gown, not someone else, don't they?

Women are also more accustomed to discussing hormone replacement therapy (HRT). HRT is much rarer for men to consider because as I said before, low testosterone is not a condition that most men address – even though they should (especially diabetics).

Nevertheless, I had already decided that if I wanted to have a happy Valentine's Day – and other "fun days" as well – to say nothing of the other important health issues related to complications of low testosterone (e.g., osteoporosis), it was time to man up and take my medicine. So, I did.

When I was called into the doctor's office, I was met by a pretty young lady who asked me quite directly, "Will you be able to give us a urine sample today?" I paused for a minute, standing there in the hallway, before replying, "No." She seemed stunned with the answer. I said "no" mainly because I was not told why I needed to do such a thing, and I object to all tests without more information. Plus, I was already getting into a foul mood, knowing what was coming.

I was hustled into an examination room. Another young lady

came in – a nurse's aide I assumed – she didn't introduce herself. Without any preamble, she said, "Take off all your clothes. I'll just turn away while you do it." I thought for a minute, then replied, "I don't think so." She too seemed stunned with the answer.

As an aside, I sure this is not a politically correct thing to ask, but why are all the assistants in the urologist's office pretty young women? I was already very self-conscious. I'd much prefer to have some old Nurse Cratchet yelling at me.

I had decided I was not going to donate, disrobe, or do anything until I had spoken with the doctor directly. I was left alone in the room for what seemed like an eternity before he finally arrived.

The Procedure

The first thing the doctor did was perform a complete physical exam. By "complete" I mean from a urologist's point of view: package check, a quick probe, and then a disconcerting discussion of the procedure to follow.

He could see I was nervous. To calm my fears, he told me he sometimes does 30 insertions a day, even opening on Saturdays to manage the demand. I'm not sure being on a medical assembly line calmed me down very much. But I got ready nevertheless.

I was lying on the examination bed in my birthday suit, on my right side with a skimpy towel barely covering the important bits, when the doctor casually informed me that I wasn't going to have a pellet inserted into my hip after all. "That's great!" I thought. "Maybe they've developed an inhalable version of the testosterone, like the flu vaccine.

My hopes were short-lived. There is no inhalable version. Instead, I was going to have 14 of the pellets inserted instead – not just one. Each pellet is about the size of a skinny elongated Tic-Tac.

The day was just getting better and better.

The doctor first froze the area by injecting my hip with a local anesthetic. "Why does 'freezing the area' burn so much?" I asked. "Because the anesthetic is acidic," he mumbled." Well of course it is – where's the fun in using something that doesn't hurt?

About a minute later he began digging a ditch in my hip with that felt like a garden trowel. Have you noticed that doctors are never gentle during operations? They poke, prod, and push your flesh around like a raw steak on the cutting board. I knew from my background reading that some people actually took videos on their phones of the operation, for later viewing and possible uploading to YouTube. I chose to look away.

While he worked, the doctor would occasionally ask, "Does this hurt?" – but only after doing it. Then he pushed seven pellets into the new tunnel in my hip. He repeated the entire procedure with a new gash and the other seven pellets, all through the same incision. Then he stitched me up, cheerily informing me that the stitches would "probably" fall off by themselves in a few days … or a few weeks. If not, "come back to see him."

The doctor left and a nurse came in to clean and bandage the wound. She then leaned on me heavily, "to compress the area on my hip, to make sure the pellets are well seated," she said. Is compressing an area that just suffered trauma really a good idea? It hurt like hell.

She told me to wait three minutes, get dressed, and then check out. "Some ice on that when you get home would help," she said. Actually, she didn't say that; she must have forgotten. And I forgot to think about it myself, which proved later to be a terrible mistake.

She did remember to tell me to pick up two prescriptions later in the day: a painkiller and an antibiotic. "Great," I thought. "I'll spend a few days in a daze with an upset stomach, and then everything will be fine. The stallion will return." Or so I thought.

Pellets Redux

The pellets didn't work for me. I had my first procedure on my left hip. The incision became infected. I took antibiotics (which made me sick to my stomach), but they didn't help. The incision area looked like someone had hidden an egg under my skin, which was hot to the touch. Being infected and a diabetic is not a good combination. My endocrinologist was not happy with the infections. He said I'd get an antibiotic resistant strain of infection and "that would be very bad" (his "clinical" medical emphasis).

I've since had the procedure done four more times. But in the "love handle" instead of the hip. It worked better than the hip in terms of having a smaller swelling under my skin. But each time I had to have more pellets inserted; the last time it was 16. Three of them popped out one a week or so after the procedure. The other two popped out while I was on a cruise; ruined my white silk shirt, and created an embarrassing blood stain. I was standing in front of the mirror, pulling it the third one with tweezers. It hurt. I felt like a cowboy digging out a bullet, except I didn't have the whiskey to dull the pain. There was still a huge lump under my skin. The incision point was reused for each procedure and has left a permanent scar on my side.

The last set never really worked properly either. My blood tests showed the positive effects lasted just a few weeks. After that, my testosterone readings were back to 450 and headed south. I decided the pellets were no longer worth it. Like a sick dog, I'm back on the shots.

What You Should Do

Take charge of your own health. This is another example of needing to be your own doctor as a diabetic. The symptoms are shared by several conditions. But when you put them all together, the diagnosis is clear. The problem with modern medicine is that you don't see a team of doctors, and they never truly share the results of their examinations.

But don't be afraid of complaining.

Don't be embarrassed.

Get your mojo back. Get into the bathtub and start enjoying life.

# # #

The Single Man's Guide to Life

June 2012

The book *Going Solo: The Extraordinary Rise and Surprising Appeal of Living Alone* by Eric Kinenberg (Penguin, 2012) is a great read. The author is a professor at NYU who writes about an unacknowledged but significant social change of the 20th and 21st centuries. In 1950, 4 million people were solo (10%); in 2011, 32 million were solo (28%), and more than 40% in major cities. It's even  higher in Europe and Japan. Today, people will spend more of their life alone than married. Note that "solo" does not mean "single." It means living alone.

For most men, life is a mystery. Any help managing some of the day-to-day issues of living alone, such as household chores, would be helpful. When women enter or leave your life, things become even more complicated.

If women don't find you handsome, they should at least find you handy.

The Red Green Show

Household Chores

This should be a very short guide because, obviously, single men should avoid household chores at all costs. Nothing good every came of men trying to do housework – just ask the wives of the married ones.

The best option is to outsource the work. Men can put up with an impressive level of disorder and various degrees of grunge and filth, but eventually we do want the place to be tidied up a bit. Well, that's what maids are for. They charge for their services, but it's a good time-for-money tradeoff. The biggest problem with getting a maid is that you need to tidy the place before they come! Who wants to do a pre-clean?

However, if your kitchen is starting to resemble a rubbish tip, if your bathroom is taking on the odor of a science experiment left out in the tropical sun for too long, or if the cat is getting a headache from banging its head against the broken pet door, then you have no choice – you can't escape household chores any longer.

The best approach is to keep things simple. Focus on the three key areas that affect you: kitchen and bathroom, laundry, and fixing the important stuff. Each of these can be done with a minimum of equipment and fuss.

Kitchen and Bathroom: Windex

There is a seemingly endless parade of ads on TV for household cleaning products. Some are specialized, such as Tidy-Bowl. Some have their own mascots or spokesmen, such as Mr. Clean. Some have industrial-sounding names that don't say anything about what they actually do, such as Formula 409. Is it a more advanced Formula-1 racing car? What happened to Formula 408? Should I wait for Formula 410 to come out?

For most men, too many choices lead to too much confusion. This is just as true for household cleaning products as it is for women in our lives. Have you ever watched single men standing in the cleaning aisles in the grocery store, looking glassy-eyed at the vast array of colored bottles, tentatively reaching out for one at random, trying to give the appearance of reading the label while in fact secretly wondering what the hell they're doing in the cleaning aisle in the first place? They usually grab a packet of Wet-Ones and scurry away.

Some maid services are old school: they swear by vinegar and water. Personally, I think they're just trying to save money. I used gallons of vinegar and water to clean the windows at McDonald's during my two-year stretch at the Golden Arches many years ago, and I can tell you it doesn't work. Well, not without so much elbow grease that your arms want to drop off, and no man wants that – it makes it hard to hold the TV remote later.

If a maid is not possible or too expensive, get yourself the all-purpose, tried-and-true, easy to find, and above all, cheapest cleaner there is: Windex. This beautiful blue liquid looks vaguely industrial, and its strong ammonia odor is quite medicinal, so we know it must work. Besides, it can be sprayed on absolutely everything with just a paper towel. It might not be the best cleaner, but it's good enough. And for most men, good enough cleaning is about as good as it's going to get.

Laundry: Time

A single man's dirty laundry never seems to be a problem – until it announces its presence with a funky odor that permeates the room. It takes a long time for men to become aware of dirty laundry because it's never in one place: there's a t-shirt on the chair, pants on the sofa, and socks scattered on the floor. If the laundry was placed in a proper place, like a hamper, it probably would get more attention – but only because it overflowed. Men know it's laundry time when the socks stand at attention by themselves.

Normal people put their dirty laundry in the washer. They know how to separate colors from whites, which detergents to use, and which clothes can go in the dryer without turning into dolls' outfits. But single men aren't normal people, and for them, the laundry room is a dangerous and dark place that's best avoided.

The easiest solution to dirty laundry is to do nothing. We know that time, some fresh air, and the occasional squirt of Windex will eventually turn dirty clothes into wearable clothes. If it passes the smell test, on it goes! The truly advanced can use this approach with a rotation method, where the clothes go from the body to the floor and back again, many times over.

When finally the clothes have such a stench that even we can't stand it, they must be cleaned. For single men, that means a trip to the dry cleaner. For everything. No mucking about with the washing machine or trips to the launderette. The dry cleaner can handle everything.

Besides, who actually understands what "dry cleaning" is, anyway? When the lady asks if you want it laundered or dry cleaned, most men just shrug. Who knows? Who cares? Just send it back on a hanger, looking vaguely crease-free, and smelling better than when we brought it in, and we're happy.

When even the dry cleaners throw up their hands, it's time to head to the store. Single men know that it's far easier to buy new underwear than it is to clean them. Ditto for socks, shirts, and sometimes even shorts and pants. If the people in the men's department at JCP don't know you by your first name yet, you're doing something wrong. (Maybe you've ventured down to the laundry room once too often.)

Fixing Stuff: Duct Tape and a Screwdriver

There's an old saying (or is it an advertisement?), "Life happens, clean it up." Sometimes more than cleaning is needed; sometimes things need to be fixed. Unfortunately.

If you're a handyman, then you're probably not reading this anyway. For the rest of us, the first thought is to call … a handyman. Good luck with that. They are fictional; they don't really exist. The guy who drives around in the "Red Barn" truck? He's either parked all the time, or he just drives around aimlessly – he never stops anywhere and fixes anything.

You could call for specialized help, like a plumber. But they're expensive. And there's that whole butt-crack issue that you'd rather avoid.

Fortunately, there's a single solution to all of your fixit needs: duct tape. It's sometimes called, "the handyman's secret weapon" (Red Green). It's the Windex of the repair world. It fixes everything.

Cracked window? Duct tape. Tear in the couch? Duct tape. Sole separating from shoe? Duct tape.

For the really difficult jobs, you can bring out the ultimate tool: the all-purpose screwdriver. It works on all screws – even ones with heads that don't match. It also doubles as a hammer.

What more do you need?

Women and the Bathroom

All lodge members recite the "Men's Prayer":

I'm a man, but I can change, if I have to, I guess.

The Red Green Show

Learning to live with a woman can be a huge challenge for the single man. It's almost like they're a different species or something.

Consider the bathroom. It's the poor man's "Man Cave." It's a functional space that also serves as a library. It's meant to be an oasis, a quiet respite from the outside world.

But when a woman enters your life, everything changes.

Toilet Paper Rolls

It seems woman are taught when they are very young that they cannot change toilet paper rolls. I think their mothers tell them they will literally die if they ever change the roll, and their mothers were told this by their mothers, and so on, throughout the generations.

No one knows where this ancestral knowledge came from.

Lately, I've found notes written in red lipstick on the empty rolls. They're cute and put a smile on my face – until I remember that someone took the time to write the note instead of just replacing the roll. Overall, I'd prefer she just replaced the roll – especially when I have to run across the house to get refills at a moment of extreme need. It just scares the cats.

And what's with the incorrect direction of the toilet paper roll on the holder? Everyone knows the roll should come from the top, towards the front, not from the bottom and to the back. How does she not know this?

Their Sixth Sense

"Scott … are you there?"

That's what I've heard from women in my life for years. It's like they have a sixth sense. The minute I go to the bathroom, they start calling my name. It doesn't matter that I'd been sitting beside them for over an hour in total silence. As soon as I leave, they want to talk.

The only thing worse than the calls is the conversations through the bathroom door. If I wanted to talk, I wouldn't be in the bathroom. I hate it when people stand right outside the door, waiting for me to come out. I feel like I'm in an airport stall, where people are yanking on the door to gain entrance – even though it's totally obvious that it's occupied.

Besides, a man's bathroom activities should not be shared – or heard. There are nasty noises and poisonous explosions that all men are familiar with, but there's just no good reason for women to know about.

The Toilet Seat

One of the oldest complaints from women is that their man fails to put the toilet seat down. What can I say? Guilty as charged. Until recently, I rarely put the toilet seat down – mostly because of the loud clang it made when striking the bowl. It never bothered when I was alone, but with a woman in the house, it's another story.

In the past, I've heard a distant splash, followed by a female voice yelling "Scott!," many times. I solved this problem by installing a "go slow" toilet seat that closes by itself very smoothly. Now I'm not startled, and neither is she.

But as the saying goes, what goes around comes around. We now have two little kittens in the house, and they are naturally curious about everything. I've told my significant other to close the toilet lid, but she keeps forgetting. Maybe the photo I took of one of the cats looking up from the bowl, doing frantic laps, will help her remember.

And why can't women be considerate and put the lid _**up**_ when they are done?

Privacy

Some people have odd views on privacy in the bathroom. I've heard that if you grew up with lots of siblings but a single bathroom, necessity forced you to share a little more than I think is healthy. I knew a family with four sisters and one bathroom, and every morning there was a production line of showering, applying makeup, getting dressed, and using the toilet. Too much sharing for me; I grew up an only child, and I value my privacy.

Sometimes I forget that not everyone shares my views on bathroom privacy. If I neglect to lock the door, that doesn't mean anyone is free to enter without knocking. Believe me, you probably don't want to see (or hear) what's going on in there.

Recently, this most basic rule was violated. The door was closed, but my girlfriend just opened it and entered without knocking. I was just getting down to business, half-standing in front of the bowl, before taking a shower. My instinctive response was to cover myself quickly.

"I heard the shower running, so I thought you were in there," she said. Then she took a closer look at me at burst out laughing. "I can't believe you're standing there, covering yourself with the Kindle!"

All I could think was, thank goodness it was the old, longer, model.

###

LIVE TURTLES

February 2013

I drive by the place every day on the way home. For a long time, it was an empty shell, the old lettering taken down, leaving only ghostly letters barely readable on the wall. Only the red and white sign was left, slowly falling apart. Each time I looked at it I felt a slight twinge of sadness. The empty sign reflected the emptiness of the building it fronted, and the emptiness I felt in my heart.

CompUSA was no more.

Hey, for a geek like me, the closing of CompUSA was a big deal!

I spent many happy hours wandering the aisles, looking at the latest hardware and software, trying out new gadgets. CompUSA was my safe haven, full of like-minded people, far removed from the chaos of places like Wal-Mart. It was geek-central, and we were proud of it.

I first went to CompUSA after Egghead closed several years earlier. With CompUSA gone I was left with Circuit City and Best Buy. Then Circuit City closed too. I was rapidly losing places to shop! Only Best Buy is left now – and they are closing some stores. (I still go to Fry's, but the closest one is in Phoenix.)

Many people lament the opening of a Wal-Mart because they fear the impact on local stores. I have no fear of Wal-Mart. The demise of Egghead, CompUSA, and Circuit City was due to a new generation of stores: online, nimble, and cheap – like Amazon.com. But I can't complain too much, or I'd be a hypocrite: I spend oodles of cash at Amazon.com too.

* * *

Imagine my surprise when one day while driving home I noticed the old CompUSA sign was completely gone. It had been replaced by a sickly-looking green and yellow contraption, with several misspelled lines of black block lettering advertising the new store.

The first line read, "Live Turtles!" My first thought was that the word "live" seemed redundant. Is there a big market for dead turtles? And just how big is the market for live turtles? What do people do with them anyway? Maybe I don't want to know.

The next line on the sign said, "We Buy Gold!" I had no gold to sell. Actually, I've never known anyone to sell his or her gold. But I'd seen the ads on late-night TV.

The sign also proudly announced, "Air Conditioned!" Really? Is air conditioning such a big thing in Florida? Are there any places left in the state without air conditioning?

What type of store sells turtles and buys gold? And has to explicitly state that it has air conditioning?

Then it finally dawned on me what type of store was opening in the old shrine: a flea market. Oh god, a flea market. The down-market equivalent of a pawn shop, thrift store, and rotting vegetable stand all rolled into one smelly mess.

* * *

How did it come to this?

How could a great place like CompUSA become a nasty place like a flea market?

For me, a technology guy, the closing of CompUSA was a blow. To see it replaced by a foul flea market is really just putting the boot in.

What used to be a bright and happy store where I once bought plastic mice has become a garish and dreary place that sells live turtles.

Now when I drive by the store on the way home I purposely look away. It pains me to see what's happened to the old place.

I wonder if Wal-Mart would consider opening a Neighborhood Market grocery store there?

# # #

Smooth Jazz

September 2013

Betty was fed up. Her cat, Jazz, was out of control. She was at her wit's end with him.

She had brought Jazz home as a young stray a few years ago. He was a bit skittish when she first brought him in, but over time he seemed to have settled into a routine. Now that Jazz was fully grown, he had become increasingly aggressive. He'd swat at her ankles when she walked by. He sometimes lunged at her face when she was holding him. He was very possessive of his food, to the point that she was afraid of refilling his water dish when he was around.

But the worst behavior was his spraying. Every day Jazz would urinate around the house. When Betty let him out, Jazz would spray the flowers, the walls, even the car wheels. The smell was overpowering. She tried swatting at him with the broom, but he'd just turn around and hiss at her.

At night, Jazz would screech and howl so loudly that Betty's neighbors were beginning to complain. Jazz sat on top of the fence post, surrounded by other cats below him that mewled and cried in a most annoying manner. It was like a feline orchestra performing the same piece, out of tune, over and over again.

While driving to work one morning, Betty came across a sign outside a vet's office that said she should neuter her pets. She didn't know what neutering meant, but made of note of the ad. At her lunch break, she called the vet and asked if neutering Jazz would put an end to his bad habits, especially the spraying. She was assured that the simple procedure would fix him. "Perfect," Betty thought. Her problems would be solved and, who knows, Jazz might be in a better mood, too. She scheduled his appointment for the next morning.

Betty had a terrible time trying to stuff Jazz into his pet carrier. When she arrived at the vet's office, her arms were a shredded mess. The vet's assistant tried to coax Jazz out of the carrier and onto the examination table, but he was having none of it. Eventually, he tumbled out when the carrier was turned on its end and shaken. "We don't normally do that," the assistant apologized. Jazz just stood on the table with his legs splayed rigid, ears back, glaring at Betty.

"The vet will examine Jazz soon, and then we'll take care of him. Why don't you leave him with us, and we'll give you a call when it's over?" the assistant asked. Betty agreed. She was glad to get out of the tiny room that had begun to smell; it made her nervous. The way Jazz was looking at her it was almost as if he knew what was coming. She still didn't know anything about the procedure but was confident the vet knew what to do. Besides, she was running late for work.

* * *

The vet called Betty late in the afternoon. "Jazz is ready to be picked up," the assistant said. "How is he doing?" Betty asked. "He's fine. Resting comfortably. Good to go."

When Betty arrived at the vet, she found Jazz already back in his carrier. He seemed quite calm. He wasn't glaring at her. He wasn't really looking at anything in particular. "Don't worry," the assistant told her. "He's still a bit sleepy from the anesthetic. He'll be back to his old self in no time." "I hope not," Betty said quietly to herself.

Jazz slept the whole night in the carrier. Betty wondered why he didn't bolt out of there at his first opportunity when they got home, but he didn't move. "Oh well, he'll come out when he's ready," she thought.

* * *

The next morning Betty's teenage granddaughter Vanessa came over for breakfast. She was familiar with Jazz's aggressive behavior and tried to avoid him whenever possible. She never had problems with any cat except for Jazz.

"Why is Jazz just sitting in his carrier, grandma?" Vanessa asked.

"I took him to the vet yesterday. They said they could fix him. You know how much trouble I've been having with him. Spraying everywhere. Whatever they did, it seems to have worked. He's been quiet as anything since we got home."

"What did they do to him?"

"I'm not sure," said Betty innocently. "I saw a sign that said something about 'neutering.' The vet said it would calm him down. I assumed he'd get some pills or shots or something. Do you know what 'neutering' means?"

Vanessa looked directly at her grandmother. "What exactly did the sign say?" Vanessa asked.

Betty looked pensive, but she also seemed to be smirking slightly. "I think it said, 'Neutering your pets makes them less nuts.'"

Vanessa was speechless. She leapt up and coaxed Jazz out of his carrier. He didn't fight or fidget. He let Vanessa pull him slowly out, onto the floor. He just stood there. He didn't make any attempt to scratch, bite, or spray. He seemed like a different cat.

"What are all those bandages doing on his back end?" Betty wondered aloud. "His fur is all shaved around there too."

"Jesus grandma, you really don't know what they did to Jazz? He's had 'the snip'! They've cut off his nuts! No wonder he's a different cat. They've turned a wild tomcat into a sleepy house cat."

Betty seemed stunned. She didn't know what to say. Vanessa just stood there, shaking her head. "I guess you can call him 'Smooth Jazz' from now on."

Betty just smiled slyly and looked down at the cat. "Exactly," she thought.

# # #

GG

September 2013

Life with a small bladder was no joke for Dick. He'd suffered his share of name calling in school: "ping pong," "gg" (for "gotta go"), and "pee machine" were some of the nicer ones. He couldn't help it if he was born with an abnormal organ.

Things didn't get much better for Dick when he grew up either. He still had to run to the toilet several times an hour. It made social situations very awkward. Going out to dinner on a date became an endless stream of excuses. He found travel difficult because he was always looking for the nearest restroom, to be used when the urge came upon him.

He'd seen several specialists. None of them could seem to diagnose his problem properly. He'd been told he had Irritable Bowel Syndrome (IBS), and Inflammatory Bowel Disease (IBD) such as Crohn's Disease or Ulcerative Colitis, even an enlarged prostate. He was pretty sure it wasn't IBS or IDB because he didn't have the other symptoms. A fun trip to the urologist confirmed his prostate was fine too. Ultimately, he was told he'd just have to learn to live with it.

* * *

Dick had tried special exercises that were supposed to strengthen your bladder. He'd read that pregnant women sometimes had similar problems. But squats didn't seem to do much for him.

He even considered going the "Depends" route, but he felt foolish doing so. He wasn't an old man, and he wasn't incontinent. He just had to go a lot. Plus they felt so uncomfortable, like wearing five pairs of underwear at the same time.

In the end, Dick settled into a routine. He tried not to drink too much, which was difficult sometimes – especially during the summer when you were supposed to stay hydrated. He also made use of a new app on his smartphone that mapped out where the closest toilets were all the time. It was a lifesaver.

* * *

No matter how hard he tried or how much he planned, sometimes Dick's bladder won. One Saturday morning he was out running errands. He was in the industrial part of the town, ironically to get some plumbing supplies, when he felt the all-too-familiar feeling of fullness start to grow within him.

He pulled off the road and into a parking lot. He whipped out his smartphone app, but for the first time, it failed him. It said there were no public toilets available within a 5-mile radius. "Shit," Dick said. "Stupid technology. Now what am I going to do?"

The urge was growing. Dick knew that soon he'd be desperate. He frantically began looking around, considering his options. He got out of the car, ready to run behind one of the stores and take care of business. Just then, he looked up and saw a sign outside a store that gave him hope.

He ran to the store and banged on their door. They were closed, but he could see the light on inside. He banged again and again. Eventually, a grumpy old man opened the door and barked, "We're closed mister."

"But I need to use your facilities. It's an emergency!" Dick implored. "Besides, your sign said you could help!" added Dick, now hopping from one foot to the other.

"What sign?"

"It's right there," Dick yelled, pointing outside. "It says, 'The best place in Brevard to take a leak.'"

"That's 'cause we're a plumbing company, pal, not McDonald's! Go somewhere else."

Dick raised his voice. "Well, my plumbing needs work. Right now it needs a flush. So LET ME IN!"

"OK, OK, calm down," the plumber said. "You can use the toilet just this once. It's the first door on the left."

Dick raced through the entrance and down the hall. "Another gg," the plumber mumbled. He looked outside at the sign and cursed – not for the first time. "What a waste of money that was. Why do we get all the crackpots?"

#

SAD HARRY

April 2014

It all started with a newspaper column and ended with a book contract. In between, there was coffee, conversation, and camaraderie.

He first contacted me in Spring 2012. He had read a few of my "Technology Today" columns in the *Florida Today* newspaper, and he had looked at my university profile online. His email said he'd like to get together – just to meet and chat.

* * *

I met him in the Sun Shoppe Café in downtown Melbourne. He was older than I expected, but fit and spry. He was also gregarious. He held forth for over an hour, regaling me with highlights of his impressive career history.

Eventually, he arrived at the reason he asked to meet with me: he wanted to know if I would consider being a reviewer for the next edition of his book, "Systems Analysis & Design." This was going to be the 10th edition of the best-selling book in the field. It had its genesis in the Shelley-Cashman series of information systems (IS) textbooks many years ago. Harry had been brought in as a co-author around 1996, and in recent years he had been the sole author.

He explained to me how the production schedule worked, how chapters were prepared throughout a 10-month period, and how he needed subject matter experts to serve as reviewers for each new edition.

He brought a sample of the book's 9th edition to give me. As I flipped through the massive volume (it has over 750 pages), I wondered how I would ever find the time to review the material over the summer. But as I was flipping through the pages another thought was occurring to me: I don't want to be a reviewer – I want to be an author.

When we parted, I told him I would consider the matter and get back to him soon. During the next few days I thought more and more about this interesting opportunity to get involved in a huge book project. But I wasn't really interested in being a reviewer. Besides, I had two books of my own I was finishing in 2012.

I declined his offer.

* * *

He seemed surprised with my decision. I explained to him that publications are the currency of academia, but being a reviewer didn't really count for anything in computing. The modest sum the publisher would pay me to act as a reviewer was barely minimum wage.

More importantly, I thought I had a lot to offer, more than being just a reviewer. I went over my publication history (I've published well over 150 academic papers), my research interests and practical experience, and outlined some possible new directions for the next edition of the book.

His response was cautious. He seemed impressed with my credentials, but my background was very different from his previous collaborators. It was clear that he cared deeply for the book, which after all these years he considered "his baby."

He said he didn't know my writing background well enough to consider my offer of becoming co-author for the next edition. It didn't matter how many accolades I could give him. I think that from his perspective, He just wasn't ready to take a leap of faith and bring me on board as the co-author without first going through the vetting process of being a reviewer.

I respected his decision, but I also was firm in my own decision. We amicably parted ways. He eventually found other people to serve as reviewers of the 10th edition of the book. It was published in March 2013 and has sold extremely well.

* * *

A year went by without any significant communication between us. Then last April Harry contacted me again, and again we met at the same coffee shop as before. He told me how well the book had been doing, how he was enjoying his free time during the brief lull between publishing one edition and planning for the next.

He eventually returned to the topic of my involvement in the book. This time he had a different proposal: would I consider being a "contributing author" to the book? I didn't quite know what this meant. He explained that a contributing author would write 2-3 chapters and would review a few chapters written by other contributors.

I'm sure he could tell by the look on my face that I was skeptical. He went on to explain that he felt he was ready to begin reducing his involvement in the book, with an end goal of retiring from the project entirely by the 12th or 13th edition. In other words, the contributing author role was a transitional one: if all went well, I would become a full-fledged co-author for the following edition. But that would be four years away, and like before, I wasn't willing to wait that long.

I declined his offer again.

* * *

One month later I was contacted again, but this time by the publisher. The book's lead production manager wanted to discuss my involvement in the 11th edition of the book. I explained to her the rationale behind my decision to decline to participate as a contributing author, just as I had explained to Harry earlier. She seemed to understand where I was coming from, and what my long-term goals were for the book.

She said Harry had had a change of heart and would consider bringing me on board as co-author for the next edition of the book, but he required evidence of my ability to master the material and write new content on a tight schedule all the while maintaining the overall voice and tenor of the lead author (himself). I could provide this evidence by agreeing to a significant writing exercise: I was to edit two chapters of the book over a six-week period. The edits would include examining all content for correctness, relevance, and timely use of examples. I was also free to add or delete any content I wished to, as long as I provided a detailed explanation for the changes I made. I also had to provide new graphics and screen shots where appropriate. After I had submitted my revised chapters, the publisher would examine them to determine whether or not I had the necessary skills to take on a bigger portion of the book.

While I was doing this, two other potential contributing authors would be doing the same thing, but on different chapters. In other words, it was a competition. The winner would become the co-author of the next edition of the SA&D book.

This time, I agreed to the offer.

* * *

I submitted my work to the publisher in late June of last year. I didn't hear anything again until the end of August. I tried contacting Harry, but he declined to speak with me during this evaluation period. I assumed it was because he wanted to remain neutral when it came to selecting the winner among the three contestants.

It turned out one person didn't submit their work on time, so the contest was between myself and one other person. The only thing I knew about him was that he had been a reviewer for the past two editions of the book. "Uh oh," I thought. "He'll certainly have a leg up on me since he's more familiar with the entire manuscript and he's already worked with Harry several times."

It was another month before the publisher told me that I had the job.

* * *

As soon as I heard the good news, I tried to speak with Harry. I was excited to begin the planning process for the 11th edition. But he still wouldn't speak with me, which I found rather odd.

I eventually talked to the publisher again a few weeks after being notified that I was to be the co-author. It turns out the reason Harry was not speaking with me had nothing to do with the writing contest and everything to do with the publisher. In July – in between submission and notification, they had declared bankruptcy! Several big-name authors had significant royalties due. All author contracts were up in the air – including Harry's.

In early September the publisher was regrouping. When they contacted me, it was a new person in charge of the book. When I finally spoke to him, he had a lot of news to impart.

Harry was out. He couldn't come to terms with the publisher, and they felt the bankruptcy and reorganization gave them the unexpected opportunity to rework a lot of their catalog. The next version of the SA&D book was in this group.

I wasn't going to be the co-author; I was going to be the lead author. Harry's name would still appear on the book's cover, to help with publicity and provide a smooth transition to the new authors involved. He would receive a reduced commission for lending his name to the project, but other than that he would not participate in any way. He had pitched a few side projects that could compliment the book, such as video lessons, but the publisher decided to make a clean break.

It was an odd situation. After I had spoken with the publisher, I tried to contact Harry again, and this time he responded. He explained the situation from his point of view. He didn't sound bitter. In many ways, this provided an exit for him, albeit a bit earlier than expected. He agreed to serve as my mentor by offering to speak with me in the coming months while I was working on the book.

So I went from reviewer to contributing author to co-author to author. Now all I had to do was sort out the contract details.

* * *

During contract negotiations I tried to contact Harry several times, between November and January. He didn't reply. I just assumed it was because he didn't want to get involved in messy financial matters – which I completely understood.

Two weeks ago the publisher sent me an email, asking to speak to me on the phone. "Uh oh," I thought again. "What's wrong now? Was the bankruptcy affecting their operations? Are they canceling the contract?"

When he called, we exchanged the usual pleasantries. He was in Vermont and complaining about the weather. He just groaned when I told him what the weather was like here in Florida.

He then broached the more sensitive topic. "Scott, I have to tell you that Harry passed away. We just found out a few days ago. Usually he checks with us in mid-March to discuss royalties; he's very meticulous about those things. When we didn't hear from him, we tried to contact him ourselves. His wife gave us the sad news. Harry passed away on January 3, 2014. It seems he was diagnosed with Stage IV cancer of the gall bladder in late 2013 and died just a few short weeks later."

I was stunned. The first thing that popped into my mind was that this was yet another example of a man who works hard all his life, finally retires to enjoy the fruits of his labor, and dies soon after.

The second thing that popped into my mind was, "No wonder he didn't reply to my email." As soon as I thought this, it seemed so trivial. But my logical mind tried to rationalize these events.

The third thing that popped into my mind was that I had lost a mentor. No longer would I have a silent partner to consult. I was truly on my own for the 11th edition of the book. I immediately felt ashamed of these selfish thoughts, but I couldn't help it. It was only when I sat down to write a note to his wife – his widow – that I realized how small my book problems were in comparison to her loss.

* * *

Work on the 11th edition of the book will be starting very soon.

I'll be writing solo. For the first time in nearly 20 years, Harry won't be involved – except in spirit. I'm confident the result will be fine, but it sure would have been nice to have an experienced mentor to offer sage advice when needed.

I will dedicate the book to SAD Harry and his legacy.

# # #

I, ROSIE

May 2014

There once was a maid named Rosie

Her specialty was cleaning floors

Her unique skills were impressive and much in demand

She was a legal immigrant from China

But went to school in Boston

Everything she learned she used to polish her craft

She started work each day at 10

Tired or not, she labored

She was meticulous and never took any rest breaks

Nobody could figure out her sweeping patterns

Occasionally she went in circles

But each room went from dusty to dirt-free

Sometimes she got stuck in a rut

Sometimes she needed to recharge

She always returned to her home at the dock

Rosie – iRosie – was an iRobot Roomba 880

Was this how Cylon's began?

Did iRosie soon become sentient and Terminate her employer?

#

I Saw Five

July 2014

You know that look you sometimes get, the look that says, "You're in deep shit," but you have no idea what you did wrong? That was the look she was giving me.

She was standing in a long queue waiting to use one of the porta-potties. She had made it to near the front; there were at least 50 people behind her. There were literally hundreds of porta-potties in a long line around the edge of the park. By chance, the line she was in was the second from the last. Beside the porta-potties was a long wooden fence.

When we first arrived, she said she had to go. I wondered why she didn't go before we left the hotel, but instead, I said "OK" and left her in search of beer. But the lines were so long it would have taken ages to get one, so instead I bought a t-shirt; at £25, it was a bargain for half the price. When I finally made my way back through the crowds to where she was, ready to show off my new purchase, her look stopped me in my tracks.

Before I could ask, "What's wrong?" she blurted out, "I've seen five penises!"

I'm not often at a loss for words, but what does one say to a statement like that? All I could stammer was, "What?"

"Right there, in front of me. Five men were peeing against the wall. They were facing sideways. I saw their fat, ugly penises!" I couldn't help but wonder if she said, "fat but ugly" or "fat and ugly"? I think it was "but," which made me wonder if it was some sort of commentary directed towards me. Putting the adjective aside, all I could say again was, "What?"

'Right there!" she pointed. "They had no shame. One of them even walked away with it in his hand, yelling to the crowd, 'Hey girls, how lucky you are to have seen this!' It was disgusting."

I finally managed to put a sentence together. "Why didn't you just look away?"

That was the wrong thing to ask. I got "that look" again. Thankfully I was spared further murderous stares when the next porta-potty became available. She climbed in and I waited. Things went downhill from there.

* * *

When she came out, she was crying. "Oh God," I thought, "what now?"

"There was no toilet paper! The seat was filthy. It was smelly. There were flies everywhere. I hate it here!" she screamed.

I went back to my default reply, "What?"

"Why did you think I'd like this terrible place?" she asked. "We normally go to the symphony! Not a low-end place like this! Have you looked at these people?"

I almost said, "I thought you'd like it because you like Metallica. We watched them on TV live from Glastonbury just a few nights ago, and you were singing along to their older songs." But I didn't say that. Instead, I just mumbled, "Sorry, I thought you'd appreciate the experience."

It was nearly time for the concert to start, so I managed to guide her towards the stage. When we rounded the corner, I knew there were going to be more problems.

* * *

It was an outdoor nighttime concert in London's Hyde Park. There were about 100,000 people there, most of them dressed in black, with lots of chains and tattoos. Many were without shirts – men and women alike. There were no seats. The crowd was already pretty rowdy. The smell of marijuana was everywhere. It was, after all, a Black Sabbath concert. What did she expect?

It was the last date on their 2014 tour, and possibly the last concert of their long career. The guitarist has cancer, and the whole band is getting on in years. And of course, the lead singer, Ozzy Osbourne, has suffered some serious damage due to many years of heavy drug use. I have to say that he sounded great though.

During the concert, Ozzy mentioned that it was his anniversary. His wife Sharon (from reality show fame) was on the side of the stage. I found it ironic that his marriage anniversary was July 4, a date we usually think of as representing freedom.

* * *

Just before the band came on stage, I started the long march towards the center of the crowd. The closer to the center we got, the harder it was to push through the throng. We eventually stopped about half way, when I heard the opening sirens of the song "War Pigs" blast from the speakers.

It soon became apparent that our current location wasn't going to work. The crowd was a writhing mass of head banging and fist pumping. Some groups were starting to dance – but it looked more like an impromptu mosh pit. Screaming drunks kept bumping into us as they tried to bash their way forward, dumping beer on us.

I could barely see the stage, but she couldn't see anything. At 5' nothing, she was looking squarely into the hairy crack of some nasty metal head. When she looked up at me, it was a repeat of "the look" that greeted me back at the porta-potty. It was time to move.

I grabbed her hand and started the long march backward, towards the edge of the crowd. It took nearly 15 minutes before we got to a small area on the grass that was not too packed. Just two guys were sitting on the ground, one throwing up and the other clutching his head. "Perfect," I thought, "this is much better."

Then it started to rain.

* * *

It was just drizzling at first, but as the concert wore on the rain got harder and harder. By the time the final song, "Paranoid," was starting, it was pouring. I agreed that it was time to go. With so many people in the park, it would take a long time to get back to Marble Arch.

It was a long walk back to our hotel. Not so much the distance, but the company. In the middle of a crowded and noisy city I was in a couple's cone of silence. When we got back to our room, we had a little chat.

She still didn't understand why anyone would like the concert. I almost said, "Well, 99,999 other people seemed to like it. Maybe the problem is with you." But again, I was able to bite my tongue and reply, "Uh hum."

The conversation circled back to the five penises. She kept saying how she didn't understand how men could do that in public. I know from personal experience that it's quite common at outdoor events, but this was her first time.

"I'm used to seeing one a day, not five," she finally said to me, ending the conversation. I fell asleep thinking that she could probably recognize those guys in a lineup — as long as they dropped their drawers.

###

ABOUT THE AUTHOR

Scott Tilley is a professor at the Florida Institute of Technology, president of the Center for Technology & Society, president of Big Data Florida, and a Space Coast Writers' Guild Fellow. His recent books include *Perseverance* (Anthology Alliance, 2017), *Surreal Technology* (CTS Press, 2017), and *Systems Analysis & Design* (Cengage, 2016). He writes the weekly "Technology Today" column for *Florida Today*. More information about his other books is available at http://www.amazon.com/author/stilley.